Easiest Guide to
Bible Study

Manny Piedad Mullaneda

Contents

Introduction...5

The Value Of Bible Study 9

Do You Know The 5 Spiritual Facts? 11

The Sacred Scriptures 15

God Unfolds The Future 19

God's Blueprint For Tomorrow..........................26

The World's Only Hope 33

Marriage And A Happy Home 39

Child Training...50

Are The Dead Alive?....................................54

Time Is Running Out....................................61

God Lives And Loves 67

The Origin Of Evil......................................75

"What Think Ye Of Christ?" 82

The Problem Of Sin 89

Sin And Its Cure 95

How You Can Become A New Person 101

The Law And The Gospel..............................108

Why Not Talk To God About The Sabbath? 114

Prayers That Are Answered 125

God's Money In My Wallet 130

The Truth About Hell 136

     Hope Beyond the Grave 142

1,000 Years Of Peace 148

How To Postpone Your Funeral 155

     Objections to the Saturday Sabbath 162

Your Day In Court 171

Does Christ Have A Church Today? 178

Why Should I Be Baptized? 187

Following Jesus All The Way 194

Introduction

Don't interpret the Bible; let the Bible interpret itself. There are about 40 Bible writers who lived at different period of time within the span of about 1,500 years. Many of them did not have the opportunity to see each other and compare notes for unity and centrality of ideas, yet surprisingly, in the whole Bible made up of 66 books, we cannot find any contradiction in the presentation of facts and truth. This shows that there is only one author of the Bible - **God!**

As you read the Bible, try to imagine that you are interviewing the writers of certain topic or subject matter. ... what they said about it.

Isaiah 28:10 says: "For precept must be upon precept, precept upon precept, line upon line, line upon line, here a little, there a little".

If one word or statement baffles you, try to look at the footnotes as reference, then find the assigned number or letter before the specific word, then look it up in the Bible, the chapter and verse referred to using the word or statement. Or be able to know more by using a concordance or Bible commentary.

It's hard to spot errors unless you know the truth. You have first to know the right answer of 5 x 5 = 25 to be able to correct if someone wrongly answers 5 x 5 = 29. Therefore fill your mind first with what is truth for you to be able to spot erroneous and distorted teachings. We can find truth in the Word of God, John 17:17 "Sanctify them by Your truth, **Your word is truth**."

It is not what one thinks that makes the fact and truth, but it is what God says. The statement of facts or truth must be based and measured by the standard. For instance the standard of time is measured not by what a man thinks, but by looking at the watch or clock; for the accurate measurement of body temperature, by the use of thermometer; the blood pressure measured by Sphygmomanometer, and the weight of things measured by weighing scale. The spiritual facts and truth is measured by what is written in the Bible. Jesus, when tempted by Satan asserted by quoting and saying: **"It is written"**. (Matthew 4:4, 7, 10)

The Holy Bible was written by holy men under the influence and inspiration of the Holy Spirit. Therefore, there is the need to pray for wisdom and guidance of the Holy Spirit as the Bible is opened for reading and understanding.

As a saying goes: "One picture is equivalent to one thousand words", so each chapter has relevant picture to portray and create vivid image on the subject matter.

To prepare the mind of the reader for every topic, effort had been made to start it with a brief story and illustration. This technique had been used by Jesus Himself when he drove home points by telling parables. The contents of this book have been arranged into question and answer format and the easy thing is that the Bible text answers are well provided following each question ... likened to spoon feeding which is ideal for busy people.

For beginners, I suggest that you open your Bible first at the table of contents, then look and get acquainted with the names of the books of the Bible from Genesis in the Old Testament to the New Testament ending the book of Revelation. If possible try to read them aloud at least three times to cater to your sense. You now employ the law of repetition: the more you repeat them the more they will register in your mind ... you read it, you say it, and hear it, and more chance for you to remember. Also take note of the pages where book names are found, then refer back to a particular book in finding the chapter and verse in case it will slip your mind. The Old Testament containing 39 books recorded events before Christ (BC), while the New Testament made up of 27 books gave account on events after the birth of Christ. (AD).

The first printing of this book had the production and circulation bringing to a total of about half a million copies sold. On account of favorable feedback and encouraging valuable testimonies, additional printing and production of this publication is now made possible with updated input and version.

As you read the following Statement of Benefits this book can offer, you will be able to:

1. **Know the ray of hope beyond the grave**
2. **Learn tips how to postpone your funeral**
3. **Discover the way to peace of mind, hope joy and love**
4. **Gain knowledge of the Bible, its theme, subject matter conveniently prepared with ready Bible texts for busy people**
5. **Grasp the open door of opportunity to accept God's offer of assurance of salvation**
6. **Face the future with confidence and without fear**
7. **Promote the building of faith, trust, obedience and Christ-like character**
8. **Find answers to life's perplexing questions.**
    "Thy word is my lamp unto my feet, and light unto my path." Psalms 119:105

The Value Of Bible Study

Of all the books ever written, none contains lessons so instructive, precepts so pure, or promises so great as the Bible. There is nothing that so convinces the mind of the inspiration of the Bible as does the reading of the Bible itself.

As guide, the Bible is without a rival. It gives a calm peace in believing, and a firm hope of the future. It solves the great problems of life and destiny, and inspires to a life of purity, patience, and well-doing. It fills the heart with love for God and a desire to do good to others, and thus prepares one for usefulness here and for the home in heaven. It teaches the value of the soul by revealing the price that has been paid to redeem it. It makes known the only antidote for sin, and presents the only perfect code of morals ever given. It tells of the future and the preparation necessary to meet it. It makes us bold for the right, and sustains the soul in adversity and affliction. It lights up the dark valley of death, and points to a life unending.

The Bible was written by thirty-five or forty men over a period of some fifteen hundred years. The books are called "word of God," or the "scriptures" (Luke 8:21; Matthew 21:42).

Easiest Guide to Bible Study consists of questions asked concerning some subjects, and answers to them from the Bible. It's a topical study of the Bible which will be found an excellent aid to private, family, and public study.

In the Bible we have a revelation of the living God. Received by faith, it has power to transform the life.

Do You Know The 5 Spiritual Facts?

Fact 1: God loves you.

"For God so loved the world, that He gave His only begotten Son, that whosoever believeth in him should not perish, but have everlasting life." John 3:16.

God wants you to live a life full of joy. "These things have I spoken to you, that your joy may remain in you, and that your joy may be full." John 15:11. But why so many problems, sufferings, worries, and troubles in this world confronting man?

Fact 2: We are separated from God because of sin.

"But your iniquities have separated between you and your God, and your sins have hid his face from you, that He will not hear." Isaiah 59:2.

Fact 3: Christ died for our sin.

"But God demonstrates His own love toward us, in that while we were still sinners, Christ died for us." Romans 5:8

Fact 4: You must receive Christ as your personal Savior.

"But as many as received Him, to them gave He power to become the sons of God, even to them that believe in His name." John 1:12

By accepting Christ in your life, what benefit can you gain? You can have eternal life! "And this is the testimony: that God has given us eternal life, and this life is in His Son. He who has the Son has life; he who does not have the Son of God does not have life. These things I have written to you who believe in the name of the Son of God, that you may know that you have eternal life, and that you may continue to believe in the name of the Son of God." 1 John 5:11-13

But how will you receive Christ? You can receive Christ through prayer and let Him come into your heart by His Spirit. Here is Christ's invitation to every sinner:

"Behold, I stand at the door and knock: if anyone hears My voice and opens the door, I will come in to him, and will sup with him, and he with me." Revelation 3:20.

Note: You can receive Christ this moment through prayer. Here is a suggested prayer:

"Dear God, I need You. I know that I am sinful. I am sorry for my sins and ask You to forgive me. I want to receive Jesus Christ as my Saviour. I confess Him as my Lord from this moment. I want to live for Him and serve Him. I thank you for hearing and answering my prayer, in Christ's name, Amen."

Having prayed this prayer, you have received Christ within your life. You are right with God. Do you like this kind of prayer? Do you want to accept Jesus as your personal Savior and Lord of your life right now? If your answer is yes, you can say the same prayer right now and give Christ the permission to come into your heart?

Fact 5: You are now a new person.

"I am crucified with Christ: nevertheless I live; yet not I, but Christ lives in me: and the life which I now live in the flesh I live by the faith of the Son of god, who loved me, and gave himself for me." Galatians 2:20

"Therefore, if anyone is in Christ, he is a new creation; old things have passed away; behold, all things have become new." 2 Corinthians 5:17

Note: The moment that you received Christ in faith, this is what happened:

1.   God forgave all your past sins.
2.   Christ came to live within you.
3.   Now you are a child of God
4.   You have just begun the greatest adventure of your life.

What should a Christian believer do to have a successful Christian experience daily?

- **Talk to God.**
  Prayer is talking to God as a friend. Cultivate this friendship. Set aside some time each day to talk to God. "Pray without ceasing." 1 Thessalonians 5:17. Just like our body, in order to live, we breath. Prayer is the breath of the soul.

- **Read the Bible.**
  "It is written, 'Man shall not live by bread alone, but by every word that proceeds from the mouth of God." We need to eat good nutritious food.

  God's word is the bread or food to our spiritual nature.

  The Bible is God's revelation of Himself to man. It reveals God's will. Study it each day. "Study to show yourself approved unto God." 2 Timothy 2:15.

  The Bereans "were more noble than those in Thessalonica, in that they received the word with all readiness of mind, and searched the scriptures **daily**, whether those things were so." Acts 17:11.

- **Witness for Him.**
  Our body needs exercise to be physically fit. The exercise in our spiritual nature is sharing our faith. Sharing this new-found faith and joy is necessary for you to grow spiritually. Tell others what Christ has done for you.

The Sacred Scriptures

How were the Scriptures given?

"All scripture is given by inspiration of God." 2 Timothy 3:16.

By whom were the men directed who thus spoke for God?

"For the prophecy came not in old time by the will of man: but holy men of God spake as they were moved by the Holy Ghost." 2 Peter 1:21.

Who, therefore, did the speaking through these men?

"God, who at sundry times and in divers manners spake in time past unto the fathers by the prophets." Hebrews 1:1.

For what purpose were the Scriptures written?

"For whatsoever things were written aforetime were written for our learning, that we through patience and comfort of the scriptures might have hope." Romans 15:4.

For what is all Scripture profitable?

"All scripture is given by inspiration of God, and is profitable for doctrine, for reproof, for correction, for instruction in righteousness." 2 Timothy 3:16.

What was God's design in thus giving the Scriptures?

"That the man of God may be perfect, throughly furnished unto all good works." Verse 17.

What does God design that His Word shall be to us in this world of darkness, sin, and death?

"Thy word is a lamp unto my feet, and a light unto my path." Psalm 119:105.

What estimate did Job place upon the Words of God?

"Neither have I gone back from the commandment of his lips; I have esteemed the words of his mouth more than my necessary food." Job 23:12.

How firm was the faith of the great Isaiah in God's Word?

"The grass withereth, the flower fadeth; but the word of our God shall stand for ever." Isaiah 40:8.

What did Christ say concerning the study of the Scriptures?

"Search the scriptures; for in them ye think ye have eternal life: and they are they which testify of me." John 5:39.

For what were the Bereans commended?

"These were more noble than those in Thessalonica, in that they received the word with all readiness of mind, and searched the scriptures daily, whether those things were so." Acts 17:11.

NOTE: "If God's Word were studied as it should be," says a modern Bible student, "men would have a breadth of mind, a nobility of character, and a stability of purpose that is rarely seen in these times. But there is but little profit derived from a hasty reading of the Scriptures. One may read the whole Bible through, and yet fail to see its beauty or comprehend its deep and hidden meaning. One passage studied until its significance is clear to the mind, and its relation to the plan of salvation is evident, is of more value than the perusal of many chapters with no definite purpose in view and no positive instruction gained."

For what enlightenment should everyone pray?

"Open thou mine eyes, that I may behold wondrous things out of thy law." Psalm 119:18.

For what spiritual gift did the apostle Paul pray?

"That the God of our Lord Jesus Christ, the Father of glory, may give unto you the spirit of wisdom and revelation in the knowledge of him." Ephesians 1:17.

Upon what conditions is an understanding of divine things promised?

"Yea, if thou criest after knowledge, and liftest up thy voice for understanding; if thou seekest her as silver, and searchest for her as for hid treasures; then shalt thou understand the fear of the Lord, and find the knowledge of God." Proverbs 2:3-5.

What is one purpose for which the Holy Spirit was sent?

"But the Comforter, which is the Holy Ghost, whom the Father will send in my name, he shall teach you all things, and bring all things to your remembrance, whatsoever I have said unto you." John 14:26.

Whom did Jesus pronounce blessed?

"But he said, Yea rather, blessed are they that hear the word of God, and keep it." Luke 11:28.

God Unfolds The Future

Ancient battle for succession of empire.

One night a minister was traveling from his home to an appointment some distance away. The night was dark and rainy. As he traveled along the highway, the headlights of his car went out. The highway over which he was traveling at that moment was wet, crooked, and dangerous.

You can well imagine the concern and fear that gripped his heart as he faced the almost impossible task of bringing his car to a safe stop without running into the deep canyon that he knew was to his right or into the steep bank to his left.

It was not until his lights went out that he realized how valuable they were and how much he depended on those lights to show him what danger lay ahead and to guide him around those treacherous turns. With the help of the Lord he managed to bring his car to a safe stop. Never again were those precious headlights taken for granted. He had learned to value them dearly.

As man speeds down the highway of life in this night of darkness, he needs to have a bright light to guide him. From every side the voice of confused humanity is heard asking the questions, "How can I know what to do and what to believe? Is there any way that I can know what the future holds for me and mine?"

How thankful we should be that God has not left us to wander alone! He has a wonderful light to guide us through this night of darkness into a kingdom of everlasting light and life. Let us now see how He has used this light to reveal where we are and where we are going.

What has God given man to guide him in this age?

"We have also a more sure word of prophecy; whereunto ye do well that ye take heed, as unto a light that shineth in a dark place, until the day dawn, and the day arise in your hearts." 2 Peter 1:19.

Through what agents does God communicate His secrets to mankind?

"Surely the Lord God will do nothing, but he revealeth his secret unto his servants the prophets." Amos 3:7.

PLEASE READ the entire chapter of Daniel 2. You will notice in this chapter that God communicated with King Nebuchadnezzar who was the ruler of the mighty Babylonian Empire. Through a dream, God outlined the future to this ancient king. Daniel 2:29. Notice how God used Daniel.

Why should this dream be of special interest to those living in these last hours?

"But there is a God in heaven that revealeth secrets, and maketh known to the king Nebuchadnezzar what shall be in the latter days. Thy dream, and the visions of thy head upon thy bed, are these." Daniel 2:28.

Who did Daniel tell the king revealed the dream to him?

"Daniel answered in the presence of the king, and said, The secret which the king hath demanded cannot the wise *men*, the astrologers, the magicians, the soothsayers, shew unto the king; but there is a God in heaven that revealeth secrets, and maketh known to the king Nebuchadnezzar what shall be in the latter days. Thy dream, and the visions of thy head upon thy bed, are these." Daniel 2:27, 28.

What had the king seen in his dream?

"Thou, O king, sawest, and behold a great image. This great image, whose brightness was excellent, stood before thee; and the form thereof was terrible. This image's head was of fine gold, his breast and his arms of silver, his belly and his thighs of brass, his legs of iron, his feet part of iron and part of clay. Thou sawest till that a stone was cut out without hands, which smote the image upon his feet *that were* of iron and clay, and brake them to pieces. Then was the iron, the clay, the brass, the silver, and the gold, broken to pieces together, and became like the chaff of the summer threshing floors; and the wind carried them away, that no place was found for them: and the stone that smote the image became a great mountain, and filled the whole earth." Daniel 2:31-35.

Who did Daniel say would interpret the dream for the king?

"This *is* the dream; and we will tell the interpretation thereof before the king." Daniel 2:36.

NOTE: God, in the interpretation of this dream, outlines the history of this world from the days of Nebuchadnezzar to the end of this world. By the use of the different metals in the image. He revealed that there would be four world empires in the succeeding years. History reveals that these were Babylon (head of gold). Medo-Persia (chest and arms of silver), Grecia (thighs of brass), and Rome (legs of iron). By this image he shows that the fourth world empire would be divided as represented by the feet of iron and clay.

What was represented by the head of gold of the image?

"Thou, O king, *art* a king of kings: for the God of heaven hath given thee a kingdom, power, and strength, and glory. And wheresoever the children of men dwell, the beasts of the field and the fowls of heaven hath he given into thine hand, and hath made thee ruler over them all. Thou *art* this head of gold." Daniel 2:37, 38.

NOTE: Babylon, with its magnificent display of wealth, was one of the wonders of the ancient world. Its beautiful buildings were interspersed with luxuriant gardens. Indeed it was the capital of the ancient golden kingdom.

How would the second kingdom, Medo-Persia, compare to Babylon?

"And after thee shall arise another kingdom inferior to thee, and another third kingdom of brass, which shall bear rule over all the earth." Daniel 2:39.

NOTE: God told Belshazzar that the Babylonians were to be succeeded by the Medes and Persians. Daniel 5:25-31.

What part of the metal man represented the third kingdom of Grecia?

"And after thee shall arise another kingdom inferior to thee, and another third kingdom of brass, which shall bear rule over all the earth." Daniel 2:39.

NOTE: *"The battles of Granicus, B.C. 334, Issus in the following year, and Arbella in B.C. 331, settled the late of the Persian Empire, and established the wide dominion of the Greeks." The Divine Program of the World's History, by H. Grattan Guinness, page 308.*

The fourth world empire, Rome, is represented by the legs of what?

"And the fourth kingdom shall be strong as iron: forasmuch as iron breaketh in pieces and subdueth all *things:* and as iron that breaketh all these, shall it break in pieces and bruise." Daniel 2:40.

NOTE: *". . . and the images of gold, or silver, or brass, that might serve to represent the nations and their kings, were successively broken by the iron monarchy of Rome." Decline and Fall of the Roman Empire, chap 38, par. 1., by Gibbon*

As the feet, part iron and part clay, represented a divided condition, what was to happen to the iron kingdom of Rome?

"And whereas thou sawest the feet and toes, part of potter's clay, and part of iron, the kingdom shall be divided; but there shall be in it of the strength of the iron, forasmuch as thou sawest the iron mixed with miry clay." Daniel 2:41.

***NOTE:** Between the years 351-476 A.D., a series of invasions by barbaric tribes from northern Europe completely overran the Roman Empire and brought it to its end. These tribes included: Saxons (English), Franks (French), Alemanni (German), Burgundians (Swiss), Lombards (Italians), Visigoths (Spanish), Suevi (Portuguese), Vandals, Ostrogoths, and Heruli*

What statement shows that the old world empires would never be welded back into one great kingdom?

"And whereas thou sawest iron mixed with miry clay, they shall mingle themselves with the seed of men: but they shall not cleave one to another, even as iron is not mixed with clay." Daniel 2:43.

Who is to set up a world kingdom in the days of the kings represented by the feet of iron and clay?

"And in the days of these kings shall the God of heaven set up a kingdom, which shall never be destroyed: and the kingdom shall not be left to other people, *but* it shall break in pieces and consume all these kingdoms, and it shall stand forever. Forasmuch as thou sawest that the stone was cut out of the mountain without hands, and that it brake in pieces the iron, the brass, the clay, the silver, and the gold; the great God hath made known to the king what shall come to pass hereafter: and the dream *is* certain, and the interpretation thereof sure." Daniel 2:44, 45.

When will Christ set up this kingdom?

"When the Son of Man shall come in his glory, and all the holy angels with him, then shall he sit upon the throne of his glory: And before him shall be gathered all nations: and he shall separate them one from another, as a shepherd divideth *his* sheep from the goats: And he shall set the sheep on his right hand, but the goats on the left. Then shall the King say unto them on his right hand, Come, ye blessed of my Father, inherit the kingdom prepared for you from the foundation of the world." Matthew 25:31-34.

In every age man has looked for a better land where the miseries and troubles of this world will be no more. Whether it be called Utopia, Heaven, Paradise, or whatever the name may be, man has longed for a place and a time when all sickness, sorrow, and death will be over.

In God's plan for this world, there is just such a heaven for the faithful. The Bible tells that Abraham, the father of the faithful, looked for that type of home. In Hebrews 11:16, speaking of the saints of old, the Bible says, "But now they desire a better country that is an heavenly, Wherefore God is not ashamed to be called their God: for He hath prepared for them a city."

We will study about that city in another lesson. Suffice it to say now that it will answer the longing of every heart and settle the problems of every sincere Christian.

As Christ was dying on the cross of Calvary there was only one bright spot in His hour of agony, that was when a dying thief turned to Him for salvation. From the depths of his contrite heart the thief cried out "Lord, remember me when thou comest into thy kingdom." Back came the promise that the thief would be with him in His kingdom.

God's Blueprint
For Tomorrow

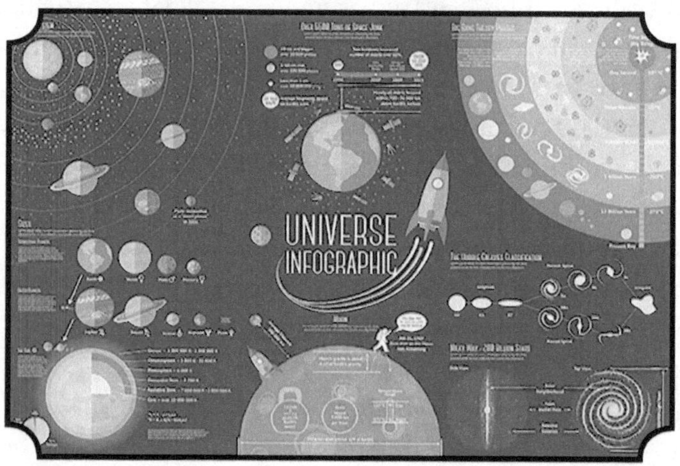

"In my Father's house are many mansions ... I
go to prepare a place for you." (John 14:2)

Billions of dollars had been spent by the nations of the world
to reach the moon. Man seems bent upon leaving this world
and reaching some other planet in the hope of finding a solution to the many problems that daily plague him.

Simply blasting out into space will not solve man's
problems. As long as the human heart is as selfish and sinful
as it is, the taint of sin and violence will be present.

How then can man find the peace and security that he
is so feverishly seeking? Is there no better tomorrow toward

which we can look? Is there no place where the plague of sickness and death will be eliminated? Is there no place where we will never grow old, where we will live in perfect peace and happiness forever?

The Bible teaches that there is such a future and such a land which God has prepared for the faithful of all ages. This is the star of hope that has given faith and courage to God's children down through the ages. This was the hope that gave the martyrs the courage to face wild animals, the promise that gave the discouraged the strength to press on, the vision that gave the grief-stricken the stamina to live another day.

From the day that Adam was driven forth from the Garden of Eden and the Tree of Life, the faithful few have longed for the time when mankind would be restored to the fellowship that man had with his Maker. God, at the gates of the garden, promised that the dominion lost by Adam would someday be restored to man by the Saviour. Genesis 3:15; Luke 19:10.

One of the last promises of the Lord was to remind the disciples of His plans to be reunited with them. Let us learn more about this wonderful city and country God has prepared for His children.

What did Christ promise He would prepare for His followers?

"Let not your heart be troubled: ye believe in God, believe also in me. In my Father's house are many mansions: if *it were* not so, I would have told you. I go to prepare a place for you. And if I go and prepare a place for you, I will come again, and receive you unto myself; that where I am, *there* ye may be also." John 14:1-3.

Who is the architect and builder of the place of which Christ spoke?

"For he looked for a city which hath foundations, whose builder and maker is God." Hebrews 11:10.

What does the Bible call the place God has prepared for His people?

"But now they desire a better country, that is, an heavenly: wherefore God is not ashamed to be called their God: for he hath prepared for them a city." Hebrews 11:16.

What name does John give to the heavenly city?

"And I John saw the holy city, new Jerusalem, coming down from God out of heaven, prepared as a bride adorned for her husband. . . . And he carried me away in the spirit to a great and high mountain, and shewed me that great city, the holy Jerusalem, descending out of heaven from God." Revelation 21:2, 10.

PLEASE READ THE COMPLETE DESCRIPTION OF THIS CITY AS FOUND IN REVELATION 21:9-27.

How does the Bible describe the features of that wonderful city?

"And the building of the wall of it was *of* jasper: and the city *was* pure gold, like unto clear glass. And the foundations of the wall of the city *were* garnished with all manner of precious stones. The first foundation was jasper; the second, sapphire; the third, a chalcedony; the fourth, an emerald; the fifth, sardonyx; the sixth, sardius; the seventh, chrysolyte; the eighth, beryl; the ninth, a topaz; the tenth, a chrysoprasus; the eleventh, a jacinth; the twelfth, an amethyst. And the twelve gates *were* twelve pearls: every several gate *was* of one pearl: and the street of the city *was* pure gold, as it were transparent glass. And I saw no temple therein: for the Lord God Almighty and the Lamb are the temple of it. And the city had no need of the sun neither of the moon, to shine in it: for the glory of God did lighten it, and the Lamb is the light thereof. And the nations of them which are saved shall walk in the light of it: and the kings of the earth do bring their glory and honour into it. And the gates of it shall not be shut at all by day: for there shall be no night there." Revelation 21:18-25.

What will be special sources of food and drink in that heavenly city?

"And he shewed me a pure river of water of life, clear as crystal, proceeding out of the throne of God and of the Lamb. In the midst of the street of it, and on either side of the river, *was there* the tree of life, which bare twelve *manner* of fruits, *and* yielded her fruit every month: and the leaves of the tree *were* for the healing of the nations." Revelation 22:1, 2.

Where are the righteous to spend the years of eternity?

"Blessed *are* the meek: for they shall inherit the earth." Matthew 5:5.

NOTE: *It is the earth made new that is eventually to become the eternal home of the saved. The New Jerusalem will be its wonderful capital.*

From what location did John say the New Jerusalem would come to this planet?

"And I John saw the holy city, new Jerusalem, coming down from God out of heaven, prepared as a bride adorned for her husband. . . . And he carried me away in the spirit to a great and high mountain, and shewed me that great city, the holy Jerusalem, descending out of heaven from God." Revelation 21:2, 10.

How will the earth be purified to receive this sinless city?

"But the day of the Lord will come as a thief in the night; in the which the heavens shall pass away with a great noise, and the elements shall melt with fervent heat, the earth also and the works that are therein shall be burned up. . . . Looking for and hasting unto the coming of the day of God, wherein the heavens being on fire shall be dissolved, and the elements shall melt with fervent heat." 2 Peter 3:10, 12.

NOTE: Read the description of this purification in Revelation 20:9.

What is God going to create after the purification of this present world?

"Nevertheless we, according to his promise, look for new heavens and a new earth, wherein dwelleth righteousness." 2 Peter 3:13.

"And I saw a new heaven and a new earth: for the first heaven and the first earth were passed away; and there was no more sea." Revelation 21:1.

What does the Bible say about the following conditions in the new earth?

Physical affliction—"Then the eyes of the blind shall be opened, and the ears of the deaf shall be unstopped. Then shall the lame man leap as an hart, and the tongue of the dumb sing: for in the wilderness shall waters break out, and streams in the desert." Isaiah 35:5, 6.

Death and sorrow—"And God shall wipe away all tears from their eyes; and there shall be no more death, neither sorrow, nor crying, neither shall there be any more pain; for the former things are passed away." Revelation 21:4.

God's dwelling place—"And I heard a great voice out of heaven saying, Behold, the tabernacle of God *is* with men, and he will dwell with them, and they shall be his people, and God himself shall be with them, *and be* their God." Revelation 21:3.

Man's occupation—"And they shall build houses, and inhabit *them;* and they shall plant vineyards, and eat the fruit of them. They shall not build, and another inhabit; they shall not plant, and another eat: for as the days of a tree *are* the days of my people, and mine elect shall long enjoy the work of their hands." Isaiah 65:21-22.

How do we become heirs of the earth made new?

"And if ye *be* Christ's, then are ye Abraham's seed, and heirs according to the promise." Galatians 3:29.

As you have read the description given in God's Word about this land and this city, you may have felt like Paul when he said, "Eye hath not seen, nor ear heard, neither have entered into the heart of man, the things which God hath prepared for them that love Him." 1 Corinthians 2:9. What more could man desire to bring genuine joy and peace into his heart and life?

Several years ago a retired gentleman received a letter from his wealthy brother in Hawaii, inviting him to come and share his wealth. The wealthy brother had prepared a mansion for him. In the invitation the promise was made that all necessities would be provided and that they would live happily together in this tropical paradise until death. It is unnecessary to tell you how long it took the brother to accept this generous offer.

God has promised far more to us than any human could offer. He promises not only freedom from sickness, fear, sorrow, and death. He has given us the assurance that His gifts will be ours if we by faith accept Christ as our Saviour and Redeemer.

If there were a land or island that could assure us of all these wonderful benefits, would we not be anxious to make any sacrifice to live there? God asks only one thing—a complete surrender of our hearts to Him. What better decision could we make than to let Jesus Christ completely control our lives today?

"Eye hath not seen, nor ear heard, neither have entered into the heart of man, the things which God hath prepared for them that love Him."

1 Corinthians 2:9

The World's Only Hope

"...While we were yet sinners, Christ died for us." Romans 5:7.

Never has the world faced so many perplexing problems that seem to have no solution. Your daily newspaper reveals a host of difficulties that man is incapable of solving.

The nations have tried in vain to resolve their differences through the United Nations. Not many of the major world problems have been solved or settled. The moral decay of mankind is apparent wherever one looks. The general confusion and perplexity in grappling with current social problems is very evident.

Many are asking, "Where can a permanent solution to these problems be found?" Your Bible holds the answer. Christ foretold the event that will resolve all of these problems of mankind. There is no other solution!

In the closing days of His ministry on this earth, nearly 2,000 years ago, Jesus talked about the day when He would be taken and crucified. The disciples of Christ would not allow themselves to believe that such a fate could ever overtake their beloved Leader. Christ knew that they would need an abiding hope in the days to come. He gave them the wonderful promise we find recorded in John 14:1-3, "Let not your heart be troubled: ye believe in God, believe also in Me. In My Father's house are many mansions: if it were not so, I would have told you. I go to prepare a place for you. And if I go and prepare a place for you, I will come again, and receive you unto Myself, that where I am, there ye may be also."

The fulfillment of this promise in the coming of our Lord the second time to this earth is the world's only hope. Let us see what the Word of God teaches concerning this wonderful event.

What does Paul call the second coming of Christ?

"Looking for the blessed hope, and the glorious appearing of the great God and our Saviour Jesus Christ." Titus 2:13.

What promise did Christ make concerning His return?

"Let not your heart be troubled: ye believe in God, believe also in me. In my Father's house are many mansions:

if *it were* not so, I would have told you. I go to prepare a place for you. And if I go and prepare a place for you, I will come again, and receive you unto myself; that where I am, *there* ye may be also." John 14:1-3.

When people talk about the second coming of our Lord being secret, what should we do?

"Then if any man shall say unto you, Lo, here *is* Christ, or there; believe *it* not. For there shall arise false Christs, and false prophets, and shall shew great signs and wonders; insomuch that, if *it were* possible, they shall deceive the very elect. Behold, I have told you before. Wherefore if they shall say unto you, Behold, he is in the desert; go not forth: behold, he is in the secret chambers; believe it not." Matthew 24: 23-26.

To what did Jesus liken the glory of His coming?

"For as the lightning cometh out of the east, and shineth even unto the west; so shall also the coming of the Son of man be." Matthew 24:27.

What will "all the tribes of the earth" see?

"And then shall appear the sign of the Son of man in heaven: and then shall all the tribes of the earth mourn, and they shall see the Son of man coming in the clouds of heaven with power and great glory." Matthew 24:30.

According to the book of Revelation, how many will be able to see Christ return?

"Behold, he cometh with clouds; and every eye shall see him, and they *also* which pierced him: and all kindreds of the earth shall wail because of him. Even so, Amen." Revelation 1:7.

What did the angelic messengers say concerning the return of Christ?

"And when he had spoken these things, while they beheld, he was taken up; and a cloud received him out of their sight. And while they looked stedfastly toward heaven as he went up, behold, two men stood by them in white apparel; which also said, Ye men of Galilee, why stand ye gazing up into heaven? this same Jesus, which is taken up from you into heaven, shall so come in like manner as ye have seen him go into heaven." Acts 1:9-11.

Who will accompany our Lord at His coming?

"When the Son of man shall come in his glory, and all the holy angels with him, then shall he sit upon the throne of his glory." Matthew 25:31.

What is the purpose of His return to this earth?

"For the Son of man shall come in the glory of his Father with his angels; and then he shall reward every man according to his works." Matthew 16:27.

What is the first event to take place at the second coming of Jesus?

"For the Lord himself shall descend from heaven with a shout, with the voice of the archangel, and with the trump of God: and the dead in Christ shall rise first." 1 Thessalonians 4:16.

What will the angels do as Christ appears in glory?

"And then shall appear the sign of the Son of man in heaven: and then shall all the tribes of the earth mourn, and they shall see the Son of man coming in the clouds of heaven with power and great glory. And he shall send his angels with a great sound of a trumpet, and they shall gather together his elect from the four winds, from one end of heaven to the other." Matthew 24:30, 31.

What will happen to the righteous who are alive at this time?

"For the Lord himself shall descend from heaven with a shout, with the voice of the archangel, and with the trump of God: and the dead in Christ shall rise first: Then we which are alive and remain shall be caught up together with them in the clouds, to meet the Lord in the air: and so shall we ever be with the Lord." 1 Thessalonians 4:16, 17.

How are the righteous changed by the coming of Christ?

"Behold, I shew you a mystery; We shall not all sleep, but we shall all be changed, in a moment, in the twinkling of an eye, at the last trump: for the trumpet shall sound, and the dead shall be raised incorruptible, and we shall be changed. For this corruptible must put on incorruption, and this mortal *must* put on immortality." 1 Corinthians 15:51-53.

__NOTE:__ "We look for the Saviour, the Lord Jesus Christ: who shall change our vile body, that it may be fashioned like unto His glorious body." Philippians 3:20, 21.

What effect will this event have on the wicked?

"And the heaven departed as a scroll when it is rolled together; and every mountain and island were moved out of their places. And the kings of the earth, and the great men, and the rich men, and the chief captains, and the mighty men, and every bondman, and every free man hid themselves in the dens and in the rocks of the mountains; And said to the mountains and the rocks, Fall on us, and hide us from the face of him that sitteth on the throne, and from the wrath of the Lamb: For the great day of his wrath is come; and who shall be able to stand?" Revelation 6:14-17.

To whom will Christ appear as Deliverer and Saviour when He comes the second time?

"So Christ was once offered to bear the sins of many; and unto them that look for him shall he appear the second time without sin unto salvation." Hebrews 9:28.

During the dark hours of World War II many Americans imprisoned by the enemy in the Philippine Islands maintained their sanity and will to live by remembering and believing a promise. That promise was made by General Douglas MacArthur when he was forced to leave them behind. He said as he left, "I shall return."

Those weary, ill-treated prisoners repeated the promise and looked forward to the day when the American Army, under the leadership of General MacArthur, would return to liberate them. They never gave up hope, for they trusted in the ability of the United States to fulfill that hope.

What a wonderful day it was when General MacArthur's soldiers and paratroopers delivered them from their prison camps. Their hopes were realized on that day.

Soon our Lord will return, for He has promised to "come again." When He comes, He will forever banish sin, suffering, and sorrow. Gone will be the world's many insoluble problems. The day of happiness and peace will have arrived!

You surely want to be ready to meet Him. Why not plan for that happy event?

Marriage And A Happy Home

A WOMAN FOR THE MAN

After creating man, what did God say?
"And the Lord God said, It is not good that the man should be alone." Genesis 2:18.

What, therefore, did God say He would make?
"I will make him *an help* meet for him." Verse 18.

NOTE: *Not a helpmeet nor a helpmate, but—two words—a help meet for him; that is, fit or suitable for him. Man's companion, or help, was to correspond to him. Each was to be suited to the other's needs.*

Could such a help be found among the creatures which God had already made?

"And Adam gave names to all cattle, and to the fowl of the air, and to every beast of the field; *but for Adam there was not found an help meet for him."* Verse 20.

A WOMAN FROM THE MAN

What, therefore, did God do?

"And the Lord God caused a deep sleep to fall upon Adam, and he slept; and he took one of his ribs, and closed up the flesh instead thereof; and the rib, which the Lord God had taken from man, *made he a woman, and brought her unto the man."* Verses 21, 22.

NOTE: *How beautiful, in its fullness of meaning, is this simple but suggestive story, at which skeptics sneer. God did not make man after the order of the lower animals, but "in His own image." Neither did He choose man's companion, or "help," from some other order of beings, but made her from man—of the same substance. And He took this substance, not from man's feet, that he might have an excuse to de grade, enslave, or trample upon her; nor from man's head, that woman might assume authority over man; but from man's side, from over his heart, the seat of affections, that woman might stand at his side as man's equal, and, side by side with him, together, under God, work out the purpose and destiny of the race—man, the strong, the noble, the dignified, woman, the weaker, the sympathetic, the loving. How* *much more exalted and inspiring is this view than the theory that man developed from the lower order of animals.*

What did Adam say as he received his wife from God?

"And Adam said, *This is now bone of my bones, and flesh of my flesh:* she shall be called *Woman,* because she was taken out of *Man.*" Verse 23.

THE TWO BECOME ONE

What great truth was then stated?

"Therefore shall a man leave his father and his mother, and shall cleave unto his wife: and *they shall be one flesh." Verse 24.*

In what words does Christ recognize marriage as of God?

"Wherefore they are no more twain, but one flesh. *What therefore God hath joined together,* let not man put asunder." Matthew 19:6.

NOTE: *Thus was the marriage institution ordained of God in Eden, before man sinned. Like the Sabbath, it has come down to us with the Edenic dews of divine blessing still upon it. It was ordained not only for the purpose of peopling the earth and perpetuating the race, but to promote social order and human happiness; to prevent irregular affection; and, through well-regulated families, to transmit truth, purity, and holiness from age to age. Around it cluster all the purest and truest joys of home and the race. When the divine origin of marriage is recognized, and the divine principles controlling it are obeyed, marriage is indeed a blessing; but when these are disregarded, untold evils are sure to follow. That which, rightly used, is of greatest blessing, when abused becomes the greatest curse.*

By what commands has God guarded the marriage relation?

"Thou shalt not commit adultery." "Thou shalt not covet thy neighbour's wife." Exodus 20:14, 17.

What New Testament injunction is given respecting marriage?

"Let marriage be held in honor among all, and let the marriage bed be undefiled; for God will judge the immoral and adulterous." Hebrews 13:4, RSV.

NOTE: By many, marriage is lightly regarded—is often made even a subject of jest. Its divine origin, its great object, and its possibilities and influences for good or evil are little thought of, and hence it is often entered into with little idea of its responsibilities or its sacred obligations. The marriage relationship is frequently used in the Scriptures as a symbol of the relationship existing between God and His people. (See Romans 7:1-4; 2 Corinthians 11:2; Hosea 2:19, 20; Revelation 19:7)

MARRIAGE WITH UNBELIEVERS

After the Fall, what sort of marriages were introduced by men, which were productive of great evil?

"And it came to pass, when men began to multiply on the face of the earth, and daughters were born unto them, that *the sons of God saw the daughters of men* that they were fair; *and they took them wives of all which they chose."* Genesis 6:1, 2.

NOTE: The "sons of God," descending from Seth, married the "daughters of men," the descendants from the idolatrous line of Cain. As a result the barriers against evil were broken down, the whole race was soon corrupted, violence filled the earth, and the Flood followed.

What prohibition did God give His people against inter-marrying with the heathen nations about them, and why?

"Neither shalt thou make marriages with them; thy daughter thou shalt not give unto his son, nor his daughter shalt thou take unto thy son. *For they will turn away thy son from following me, that they may serve other gods: so* will the anger of the Lord be kindled against you, and destroy thee suddenly." Deuteronomy 7:3, 4.

NOTE: *Intermarriage with the ungodly was the mistake made by the professed people of God before the Flood, and God did not wish Israel to repeat that folly.*

What instruction is given in the New Testament regarding partnership with unbelievers?

"Be ye not unequally yoked together with unbelievers: for what fellowship hath righteousness with unrighteousness? and what communion hath light with darkness? and what concord hath Christ with Belial? or what part hath he that believeth with an infidel? and what agreement hath the temple of God with idols? for ye are the temple of the living God." 2 Corinthians 6:14-16.

NOTE: *This instruction forbids all compromising partnerships. Marriage of believers with unbelievers has ever been a snare by which Satan has captured many earnest souls who thought they could win the unbelieving, but in most cases have themselves drifted away from the moorings of faith into doubt, backsliding, and loss of religion. It was one of Israel's constant dangers, against which God warned them repeatedly. "Give not your daughters unto their sons, neither take their daughters unto your sons, nor seek their peace [by such compromise] or their wealth for ever." Ezra 9:12. (See also Exodus 34:14-16; Judges 14:1-3; Ezra 9 and 10; Nehemiah 13:23-27.) Even Solomon* *fell before the influence of heathen wives. Concerning him the inspired Word has left this melancholy record: "His wives turned away his heart after other gods." 1 Kings 11:4. No Christian can marry an unbeliever without running serious risk, and placing himself upon the enemy's ground. The Scriptures do not advocate separation after the union has been formed (see 1 Corinthians 7:2-16), but good sense should teach us that faith can best be maintained, and domestic happiness best ensured, where both husband and wife are believers, and of the same faith. Ministers and parents, therefore, should warn the young against all improper marriages.*

What instruction did Abraham give his servant Eliezer when sending him to select a wife for his son Isaac?

"Thou shalt take a wife for my son *of my kindred, and of my father's house."* Genesis 24:40.

NOTE: *This passage indicates that in early Bible times parents generally had more to do in the selection of life companions for their children than they commonly have now. Young people who are wise will seek the advice and counsel of their parents, and above all, seek to know the will of God, before entering upon this important relationship, with its grave responsibilities and its momentous consequences.*

MARRIAGE AND DIVORCE

For how long does marriage bind the contracting parties?

"For the woman which hath an husband is bound by the law to her husband *so long as he liveth."* Romans 7:2 (See 1 Corinthians 7:39.)

What only does Christ recognize as proper ground for dissolving the marriage relationship?

"Whosoever shall put away his wife, *except it be for fornication,* and shall marry another, committeth adultery." Matthew 19:9.

NOTE: *Civil laws recognize other reasons as justifiable causes for separation, such as extreme cruelty, habitual drunkenness, or other like gross offenses; but only one offense, according to Christ, warrants the complete annulment of the marriage tie.*

THE COMPLETE HOME

Where and by whom were the foundations of the home laid?

"And *the Lord God* planted a garden eastward *in Eden;* and *there* he put the man whom he had formed." Genesis 2:8.

In making this home, what besides man was needed?

"And the Lord God said, It is not good that the man should be alone; I will make him *an help meet [one adapted or suitable] for him."* Verse 18.

After creating Adam and Eve, what did God say to them?

"And God blessed them, and God said unto them, *Be fruitful, and multiply, and replenish the earth."* Genesis 1:28.

To what are the wife and children of the man who fears the Lord likened?

"Happy shalt thou be, and it shall be well with thee. Thy wife shall be as a *fruitful vine* by the sides of thine house: Thy children like *olive plants* round about thy table." Psalm 128:2, 3.

What are children declared to be?

"Lo, children are *an heritage of the Lord.*" Psalm 127:3. "Children's children are the *crown of old men;* and the glory of children are their fathers." Proverbs 17:6.

RELATIONSHIP OF HUSBAND AND WIFE

How should the wife relate herself to her husband?

"Wives, *submit yourselves* unto your own husbands, as unto the Lord. For the husband is the head of the wife, even as Christ is the head of the church." Ephesians 5:22, 23.

And how should husbands regard their wives?

"*Husbands, love your wives, even as Christ also loved the church, and gave himself for it. . . . So ought men to love their wives as their own bodies. He that loveth his wife loveth himself. . . . Let every one of you in particular so love his wife even as himself; and the wife see that she reverence her husband.*" Verses 25-33.

Against what are husbands cautioned?

"Husbands, love your wives, and be not bitter against them." Colossians 3:19.

Why should wives be in subjection to their husbands?

"*Likewise, ye wives, be in subjection to your own husbands; that, if any obey not the word, they also may without the word be won by the conversation [manner of life] of the wives.*" 1 Peter 3:1.

Why should husbands be considerate of their wives?

"Likewise, ye husbands, dwell with them according to knowledge, giving honour unto the wife, as unto the weaker vessel, and as being heirs together of the grace of life; *that your prayers be not hindered." Verse 7.*

PARENTS AND CHILDREN

Why should children obey their parents?

"Children, obey your parents in the Lord: *for this is right."* Ephesians 6:1.

How should parents bring up their children?

"And, ye fathers, provoke not your children to wrath: but *bring them up in the nurture and admonition of the Lord."* Verse 4.

Why should fathers not provoke their children to anger?

"Fathers, provoke not your children to anger, *lest they be discouraged." Colossians 3:21.*

By what means may the mother bind the hearts of the loved ones at home together?

"She openeth her mouth with wisdom; and in her tongue is the *law of kindness."* Proverbs 31:26.

NOTE: "We want to get into the hearts of our children if we hold them, and help them, and bless them, and take them to heaven with us."—FRANCES MURPHY.

How will such a mother be regarded?

"Her children arise up, and *call her blessed;* her husband also, and *he praiseth her."* Verse 28.

NOTE: "Show me a loving husband, a worthy wife, and good children, and no pair of horses that ever flew along the road could take me in a year where I could see a more pleasing sight. Home is the grandest of all institutions."—SPURGEON.

How faithfully should parents teach the precepts and commandments of God to their children?

"And thou shalt teach them diligently unto thy children, and shalt talk of them when thou sittest in thine house, and when thou walkest by the way, and when thou liest down, and when thou risest up." Deuteronomy 6:7.

NOTE: *"The home is the child's first school, and it is here that the foundation should be laid for a life of service. Its principles are to be taught not merely in theory. They are to shape the whole life training. . . .*

"Such an education must be based upon the word of God. Here only are its principles given in their fullness. The Bible should be made the foundation of study and of teaching. The essential knowledge is a knowledge of God and of Him whom He has sent."—E. G. White, Your Home and Health, pp. 72-75.

"Continue thou in the things which thou hast learned and hast been assured of, knowing of whom thou hast learned them; and that from a child thou hast known the holy scriptures, which are able to make thee wise unto salvation through faith which is in Christ Jesus." 2 Timothy 3:14, 15.

"A church within a church, a republic within a republic, a world within a world, is spelled by four letters—home! If things go right there, they go right everywhere; if things go wrong there, they go wrong everywhere. The door-sill of the dwelling-house is the foundation of church and state. . . . In other words, domestic life overarches and undergirds all other life. . . . First, last, and all the time, have Christ in your home."—TALMAGE.

What is the great secret of a happy home?

"Better is a dinner of herbs where *love is,* than a stalled ox and hatred therewith." Proverbs 15:17.

"Religion is love, and a religious home is one in which love reigns."

J. R. Miller

Child Training

WHAT TO TEACH CHILDREN

How should parents train their children?

"Train up a child *in the way he should go; and when he is old, he will not depart from it.*" Proverbs 22:6. "And, ye fathers, provoke not your children to wrath: but *bring them up in the nurture and admonition of the Lord.*" Ephesians 6:4.

How diligently should parents teach children God's Word?

"*These words, which I command thee this day, shall be in thine heart: and thou shalt teach them diligently unto thy children.*" "*Ye shall teach them your children, speaking of them when thou sittest in thine house, and when thou walkest by the way, when thou liest down, and when thou risest up.*" Deuteronomy 6:6, 7; 11:19.

What high ideal should be placed before the young?

"Let no man despise thy youth; but *be thou an example of the believers* in word, in conversation, in charity, in spirit, in faith, in purity." 1 Timothy 4:12.

What duty does God require of children?

"Honour thy father and thy mother." Exodus 20:12.

CORRECTING CHILDREN— CAUTION TO PARENTS

How should the youth be taught to regard the aged?

"Thou shalt *rise up before the hoary head,* and *honour the face of the old man,* and fear thy God: I am the Lord." Leviticus 19:32.

What are some good fruits of proper child training?

"Correct thy son, and he shall give thee rest; yea, he shall give delight unto thy soul." Proverbs 29:17.

What will result if correction is withheld?

"The rod and reproof give wisdom: but *a child left to himself bringeth his mother to shame."* Verse 15. (See Proverbs 22:15.)

Does proper correction evidence a want of parental love?

"He that spareth his rod hateth his son: but *he that loveth him chasteneth him betimes."* Proverbs 13:24.

NOTE: One Christian mother writes thus concerning the importance of child training: "Children who are allowed to come up to manhood or womanhood with the will undisciplined and the passions uncontrolled, will generally in after-life pursue a course which God condemns. The neglect of parents to properly discipline their children has been a fruitful source of evil in many families. The youth have not been restrained as they should have been. Parents have neglected to follow the directions of the Word of God in this matter, and the children have taken the reins of government into their own hands. The consequence has been that they have generally succeeded in ruling their parents, instead of being under their authority. False ideas and a foolish, misdirected affection have nurtured traits which have made the children unlovely and unhappy, have embittered the lives of the parents, and have extended their baleful influence from generation to generation. Any child that is permitted to have his own way will dishonor God and bring his father and mother to shame."

Whom does the Lord chasten?

"For whom the Lord *loveth* he chasteneth, and scourgeth every son whom he receiveth." Hebrews 12:6.

NOTE: *From this we may learn that all child training should be done in love, and that proper child training is an evidence of true love.*

Against what evil should fathers guard?

"Fathers, *provoke not your children to anger,* lest they be discouraged." Colossians 3:21.

NOTE: *Correction should never be given in anger, for anger in the parents stirs up anger in the child. It is well to pray with a child before correcting him, and frequently mild but faithful instruction, admonition, and prayer are all the training necessary—are, in fact, the best training that can be given. But in any case of perverseness, stubbornness, or willful disobedience the correction, whatever it may be, should be persisted in until the child yields submissively to the will and wishes of the parent. It is best generally, that correction should be done in private, as* *this tends to preserve the self-respect of the child, a very important element in character building. No correction or training should be violent or abusive, or given for the purpose of breaking the will of the child, but rather to direct the will, bring it into proper subjection, and the child to a realizing sense of what is right and duty.*

How are the present effects and future results of God's chastisement contrasted?

"Now no chastening for the present seemeth to be joyous but *grievous:* nevertheless afterward it *yieldeth the peaceable fruit of righteousness* unto them which are exercised thereby." Hebrews 12:11.

Why did God reprove Eli?

"In that day I will perform against Eli all things which I have spoken concerning his house: when I begin, I will also make an end. For I have told him that I will judge his house for ever for the iniquity which he knoweth; *because his sons made themselves vile, and he restrained them not.*" 1 Samuel 3:12, 13.

What is to be one of the prominent sins of the last days?

"For men shall be lovers of their own selves, covetous, boasters, proud, blasphemers, *disobedient to parents,* unthankful, unholy." 2 Timothy 3:2.

"How excellent is thy lovingkindness, O God! therefore the children of men put their trust under the shadow of thy wings."

Psalm 36:7.

Are The Dead Alive?

A small lad, making his way through a graveyard, stopped to read an inscription on the headstone marking a grave. He was intrigued by the following epitaph: "Stop, my friend, as you go by. As you are now, so once was I. As I am now, you soon shall be. So prepare yourself to follow me." The boy stood there for some time thinking. Then, taking a piece of crayon from his pocket, he wrote this message: "To follow you I'm not content, until I know which way you went." The message he wrote may not be good poetry, but the thought expressed is a profound one.

Every person should be interested in what will happen to him at death. He should know just where he will go when the last breath leaves his body, for everyone faces death, sooner or later.

The Bible pictures death as an enemy of mankind. God tells us that the last of our enemies to be destroyed is death. Death came into the world because of the disobedience of Adam and Eve. In Romans 5:12 Paul writes, "Wherefore, as by one man sin entered into the world, and death by sin; and so death passed upon all men, for that all have sinned." God had provided that man should eat of the tree of life and live forever. When man disobeyed God, he was deprived of this privilege. Genesis 3:22, 23.

Ever since death entered this world, Satan has worked long and hard to confuse the mind of man and to keep him from understanding God's plan for giving us eternal life. The Bible teaches in a simple way what God wants us to know about death and its remedy. When we understand the Bible teaching regarding death and the resurrection, the sting of death is less painful.

Let us lay aside all preconceived ideas and let God guide us now as we study from His Book what He has to say about death.

What two elements were used by God to make man a living soul?

"And the Lord God formed man *of* the dust of the ground, and breathed into his nostrils the breath of life; and man became a living soul." Genesis 2:7.

NOTE: *God did not put a living soul into man, but the combination of life and body made man a living soul.*

What happens to the body of man at death?

"In the sweat of thy face shalt thou eat bread, till thou return unto the ground; for out of it wast thou taken; for dust thou art, and unto dust shalt thou return." Genesis 3:19.

"Then shall the dust return to the earth as it was: and the spirit shall return unto God who gave it." Ecclesiastes 12:7.

What happens to the "breath of life," or the "spirit," at death?

"Then shall the dust return to the earth as it was: and the spirit shall return unto God who gave it." Ecclesiastes 12:7.

NOTE: This spark of life is called the spirit or breath of life. These terms are used interchangeably and denote only the element of life, not consciousness or intelligence. See the following texts: Job 27:3, Genesis 2:7.

Where do all the dead go at the time of death?

"For I know *that* thou wilt bring me *to* death, and *to* the house appointed for all living." Job 30:23.

"If I wait, the grave is mine house: I have made my bed in the darkness." Job 17:13.

At death, what happens to man's ability to think?

"Put not your trust in princes, *nor* in the son of man, in whom *there is* no help. His breath goes forth, he returneth to his earth; in that very day his thoughts perish." Psalm 146:3, 4.

How much does man know during the time that he is dead?

"For the living know that they shall die: but the dead know not any thing, neither have they any more a reward; for the memory of them is forgotten. Also their love, and their hatred, and their envy, is now perished; neither have they any more a portion for ever in any *thing* that is done under the sun." Ecclesiastes 9:5, 6.

How much of man's knowledge remains when he is in the grave?

"Whatsoever thy hand findeth to do, do it with thy might; for there is no work, nor device, nor knowledge, nor wisdom, in the grave, whither thou goest." Ecclesiastes 9:10.

What does the Bible say about the possibility of the dead praising the Lord?

"The dead praise not the Lord, neither any that go down into silence." Psalm 115:17.

"For in death there is no remembrance of thee: in the grave who shall give thee thanks?" Psalm 6:5.

What did Jesus call death?

"These things said he: and after that he saith unto them, Our friend Lazarus sleepeth; but I go, that I may awake him out of sleep. Then said his disciples, Lord, if he sleep, he shall do well. Howbeit Jesus spake of his death: but they thought that he had spoken of taking of rest in sleep. Then said Jesus unto them plainly, Lazarus is dead." John 11:11-14.

If there were no resurrection, what would happen to all of the dead?

"For if the dead rise not, then is not Christ raised: And if Christ be not raised, your faith is vain; ye are yet in your sins. Then they also which are fallen asleep in Christ are perished." 1 Corinthians 15:16-18.

Because Christ rose from the dead, when can we look forward to the resurrection of our loved ones?

"For as in Adam all die, even so in Christ shall all be made alive. But every man in his own order: Christ the firstfruits; afterward they that are Christ's at his coming." 1 Corinthians 15:22, 23.

How many will be resurrected, according to the Bible?

"Marvel not at this: for the hour is coming, in the which all that are in the graves shall hear his voice, And shall come forth; they that have done good, unto the resurrection of life; and they that have done evil, unto the resurrection of damnation." John 5:28, 29.

What does Paul say will happen to the righteous dead at Christ's second coming?

"For the Lord himself shall descend from heaven with a shout, with the voice of the archangel, and with the trump of God: and the dead in Christ shall rise first: Then we which are alive and remain shall be caught up together with them in the clouds, to meet the Lord in the air: and so shall we ever be with the Lord." 1 Thessalonians 4:16, 17.

How will all of the righteous be changed at the coming of Christ?

"Behold, I shew you a mystery; We shall not all sleep, but we shall all be changed, in a moment, in the twinkling of an eye, at the last trump: for the trumpet shall sound, and the dead shall be raised incorruptible, and we shall be changed. For this corruptible must put on incorruption, and this mortal *must* put on immortality. So when this corruptible shall have put on incorruption, and this mortal shall have put on immortality, then shall be brought to pass the saying that is written, Death is swallowed up in victory." 1 Corinthians 15:51-54.

How will the bodies of the redeemed be changed?

"For our conversation is in heaven; from whence also we look for the Saviour, the Lord Jesus Christ: Who shall change our vile body, that it may be fashioned like unto his glorious body, according to the working whereby he is able even to subdue all things unto himself." Philippians 3:20, 21.

Who alone will enjoy eternal life?

"For God so loved the world, that he gave his only begotten Son, that whosoever believeth in him should not perish, but have everlasting life." John 3:16.

NOTE: Man is mortal. Job 4:17. Only God has immortality. 1 Timothy 6:15, 17. Eternal life is the gift of God only to those who believe in Christ.

Only through Christ do we have the hope of future life. If God had not been willing to give His Son to die in our stead, death would have been the end of man's existence. Since Christ came, lived a perfect life of obedience, died in our place, and was resurrected, we now have the hope of a future life—a glorious life in which sin, sickness, sorrow, and death will be forever banished.

God's plan for those who die before the coming of the Lord is well illustrated in the experience of Lazarus. Jesus told His disciples that Lazarus was asleep and then proceeded to show that He was speaking of the death of His friend as a sleep. When Christ told Martha that Lazarus would live again, Martha said, "I know that he shall rise again in the resurrection at the last day." John 11:24. She had listened to Christ's teachings. She looked forward to the final resurrection. Christ then demonstrated what will happen when He returns the second time. Standing at the open door of the tomb, He called, "Lazarus, come forth." The Bible says that

Lazarus obeyed the voice of the Lifegiver and came forth, still bound in his grave clothes.

Later Christ proved that He had gained the victory over death by His own resurrection. This was the sign that His sacrifice had been accepted by His Father, and that He had gained the right to abolish death and the devil, for the Bible tells us, "Forasmuch then as the children are partakers of flesh and blood, He also Himself likewise took part of the same; that through death He might destroy him that had the power of death, that is, the devil." Hebrews 2:14.

Thank God the victory has been gained and it can be ours by accepting the Victor as our Saviour. His death paid the price for our sins. Won't you accept Him today and be assured of eternal life at the soon coming of our Lord?

"For God so loved the world, that He gave His only begotten Son, that whosoever believeth in Him should not perish, but have everlasting life."

John 3:16

Time Is Running Out

It is not uncommon for a man to say, as he looks at the color of the sky before dusk, "It looks as if we might be in for a storm." Christ spoke of this very thing when He said, "When it is evening, ye say, It will be fair weather: for the sky is red. And in the morning, It will be foul weather today: for the sky is red and lowering. O ye hypocrites, ye can discern the face of the sky; but can ye not discern the signs of the times?" Matthew 16:2, 3.

Men have now developed scientific ways of foretelling weather by observing certain signs in the atmosphere. With the help of science, weather forecasting has become quite accurate. Just so, other scientific instruments save time and labor, yet most people take less time to study the Scriptures which present the signs that Christ said would foretell His coming and the end of the world.

Occasionally a misguided soul will arise to predict the exact date of the end of all things. A few people will be concerned, and some will anxiously watch the outcome of the prediction. When the time comes and nothing happens, many will breathe a sigh of relief and settle back into their regular routines.

Each crisis and unfulfilled human prediction has the effect of hardening the skeptic in his unbelief. Like the men who heard the boy cry "Wolf, wolf!" we have adjusted to such spectacular events as atomic explosions and great earthquakes.

So, few are aware of the many signs that God has hung along the highway of life to remind all that we are nearing the end of man's rebellion against his Maker. Christ has given a number of specific signs to show without question that time is short and His coming is near. He does this so all can make necessary preparation for the greatest event in the history of the world.

Who only knows the exact day and hour of the end of this world and the coming of Christ?

"But of that day and hour knoweth no man, no, not the angels of heaven, but my Father only." Matthew 24:36.

Is there any way by which we can know when the end is near?

"Now learn a parable of the fig tree; When his branch is yet tender, and putteth forth leaves, ye know that summer *is* nigh: So likewise ye, when ye shall see all these things, know that it is near, *even* at the doors." Matthew 24:32, 33.

What will the nations be doing just before the coming of Christ?

"And ye shall hear of wars and rumours of wars: see that ye be not troubled: for all these things must come to pass, but the end is not yet. For nation shall rise against nation, and kingdom against kingdom: and there shall be famines, and pestilences, and earthquakes, in divers places." Matthew 24:6, 7.

"Proclaim ye this among the Gentiles; Prepare war, wake up the mighty men, let all the men of war draw near; let them come up: Beat your plowshares into swords, and your pruninghooks into spears: let the weak say, I *am* strong." Joel 3:9-12.

What signs in the natural world herald the coming of Jesus?

"And great earthquakes shall be in divers places, and famines, and pestilences; and fearful sights and great signs shall there be from heaven." Luke 21:11.

What terms are used to describe the anxiety and trouble that will exist among the nations just before the end?

"And there shall be signs in the sun, and in the moon, and in the stars; and upon the earth distress of nations, with perplexity; the sea and the waves roaring; Men's hearts failing them for fear, and for looking after those things which are coming on the earth: for the powers of heaven shall be shaken." Luke 21:25, 26.

What are the signs that will be seen in the financial or economic world?

"Go to now, *ye* rich men, weep and howl for your miseries that shall come upon *you*. Your riches are corrupted, and your garments are motheaten. Your gold and silver is cankered; and the rust of them shall be a witness against you, and shall eat your flesh as it were fire. Ye have heaped treasure together for the last days. Behold, the hire of the labourers who have reaped down your fields, which is of you kept back by fraud, crieth: and the cries of them which have reaped are entered into the ears of the Lord of sabaoth. Ye have lived in pleasure on the earth, and been wanton; ye have nourished your hearts, as in a day of slaughter. Ye have condemned *and* killed the just; *and he* doth not resist you. Be patient therefore, brethren, unto the coming of the Lord. Behold, the husbandman waiteth for the precious fruit of the earth, and hath long patience for it, until he receive the early and latter rain. Be ye also patient; stablish your hearts for the coming of the Lord draweth nigh." James 5:1-8.

What message will the nations be proclaiming, and what will actually happen?

"For when they shall say, Peace and safety; then sudden destruction cometh upon them, as travail upon a woman with a child; and they shall not escape. But ye, brethren, are not in darkness, that that day should overtake you as a thief." 1 Thessalonians 5:3, 4.

What are some of the signs of moral deterioration in the last days?

"This know also, that in the last days perilous times shall come. For men shall be lovers of their own selves, covetous, boasters, proud, blasphemers, disobedient to parents, unthankful, unholy, without natural affection, trucebreakers, false accusers, incontinent, fierce, despisers of those that are good, traitors, heady, highminded, lovers of pleasures more than lovers of God: Having a form of godliness, but denying the power thereof: from such turn away." 2 Timothy 3:1-5.

What did Daniel say would happen in the time of the end?

"But thou, O Daniel, shut up the words, and seal the book, even to the time of the end: many shall run to and fro, and knowledge shall be increased." Daniel 12:4.

What will the scoffers in the religious world be saying at this time?

"Knowing this first, that there shall come in the last days scoffers, walking after their own lusts, and saying, Where is the promise of his coming? for since the fathers fell asleep, all things continue as *they were* from the beginning of the creation." 2 Peter 3:3, 4.

What must be proclaimed in all of the world before the Lord can return?

"And this gospel of the kingdom shall be preached in all the world for a witness unto all nations; and then shall the end come." Matthew 24:14.

When we see all these signs being fulfilled, what are we to do?

"And when these things begin to come to pass, then look up, and lift up your heads; for your redemption draweth nigh." Luke 21:28.

How can we prepare for that day?

"Watch ye therefore, and pray always, that ye may be accounted worthy to escape all these things that shall come to pass, and to stand before the Son of man." Luke 21:36.

For 120 years God warned the world that existed before the Flood of coming destruction. Many refused to believe that such a catastrophe could happen. Many said that it was an impossibility. Noah predicted that it would happen, and to show his faith, he invested his time and fortune in building a gigantic boat.

Only eight people cared enough about being saved to take advantage of the means of salvation that God had provided. Noah, his wife, three sons, and their wives were the only human beings who responded to God's message.

Christ said that earth's last generation would be like the one of Noah's day. "But as the days of Noe [Noah] were, so shall also the coming of the Son of man be. For as in the days that were before the Flood they were eating and drinking, marrying and giving in marriage, until the day that Noe [Noah] entered into the ark, and knew not until the Flood came, and took them all away; so shall also the coming of the Son of man be." Matthew 24:37-39.

What a deliverance for those who were ready! However, many were so busy with the cares and pleasures of life that they did not take time to prepare. The same danger faces each of us. We can become so engrossed in the affairs of this present world that we may fail to prepare for the coming of Jesus. Would we not be wise to heed the admonition of Jesus given in Matthew 24:44?

God Lives And Loves

There was a time when nearly all those living in Christian countries believed in God. An atheist was the exception. Times are changing. Men's concepts of God are changing. Many today think it a mark of scholarship to deny the existence of God. A great political system attempts to remove the very knowledge of God from men's minds to advance its own concepts. Even some who profess Christianity claim that "God is dead."

Can we know that there is a supreme, intelligent Being whom we call God? It is in the Bible that God has most fully revealed Himself. Let us look at three Bible texts as we begin our study.

1. "For what can be known about God is plain to them, because God has shown it to them. Ever since the creation of the world His invisible nature, namely, His eternal power and deity, has been clearly perceived in the things that have been made." Romans 1:19, 20. Revised Standard Version. This text states that the natural world plainly testifies to the existence and creative power of God.

2. "Upholding all things by the word of His power." Hebrews 1:3. This second text affirms that God, through Jesus Christ His Son, upholds or maintains all created things. For example, it is God who keeps all the heavenly bodies moving in their appointed orbits.

3. "For in Him we live, and move, and have our being." Acts 17:28. The third great Bible truth on this subject informs us that all life is sustained by God. There must be a source for life, and God is that ultimate source.

What positive statement does the Bible make about the existence of God?

"But there is a God in heaven that revealeth secrets, and maketh known to the king Nebuchadnezzar what shall be in the latter days. Thy dream, and the visions of thy head upon thy bed, are these." Daniel 2:28.

What fundamental declaration is made by the Ruler of the universe?

"I *am* the Lord, and *there is* none else, *there is* no God beside me: I girded thee, though thou hast not known me: That they may know from the rising of the sun, and from the west, that *there is* none beside me. I *am* the Lord, and *there is* none else." Isaiah 45:5, 6.

"Know therefore this day, and consider *it* in thine heart, that the Lord he *is* God in heaven above, and upon the earth beneath: *there is* none else." Deuteronomy 4:39.

Upon what does God base His claim to our worship and allegiance?

"For thus saith the Lord that created the heavens: God himself that formed the earth and made it, he hath established it, he created it not in vain, he formed it to be inhabited: I *am* the Lord, and *there is* none else." Isaiah 45:18.

As we look up into the wonderful starry heavens, what do they declare?

"The heavens declare the glory of God, and the firmament sheweth his handywork. Day unto day uttereth speech, and night unto night sheweth knowledge. *There is* no speech nor language, *where* their voice is not heard." Psalm 19:1-3.

NOTE: The countless millions of gigantic suns and planets orbiting space in orderly precision all testify to the presence of a mighty Creator, who also guides these heavenly bodies in their courses. Inanimate material substances have no intelligence to create and observe the laws of nature.

What evidences of the guidance of a divine being are seen in the animal kingdom?

(a) "I will praise thee; for I am fearfully and wonderfully made: marvellous are thy works; and that my soul knoweth right well." Psalm 139:14.

(b) "Gavest thou the goodly wings unto the peacocks? or wings and feathers unto the ostrich?" Job 39:13.

(c) "As an eagle stirreth up her nest, fluttereth over her young, spreadeth abroad her wings, taketh them, beareth them on her wings: so the Lord alone did lead him, and there was no strange god with him." Deuteronomy 32:11, 12.

(d) "Yea, the stork in the heaven knoweth her appointed times; and the turtle and the crane and the swallow observe the time of their coming; but my people know not the judgment of the Lord." Jeremiah 8:7.

In what language does Job assure us that it is God who guides the instinctive behavior of birds and animals?

"But ask now the beasts, and they shall teach thee; and the fowls of the air, and they shall tell thee. Or speak to the earth, and it shall teach thee; and the fishes of the sea shall declare unto thee. Who knoweth not in all these that the hand of the Lord hath wrought this? In whose hand *is* the soul of every living thing, and the breath of all mankind." Job 12:7-10.

NOTE: *The marvelous behavior of certain birds and animals clearly shows that they are guided by a divine intelligence. The activities of the beavers, the miraculous flight of migratory birds over thousands of miles of land and uncharted seas, the ingenious work of bees and ants, are but a few examples of this guidance.*

In addition to the power of creation, what other supernatural gift does God claim to possess?

"Remember the former things of old: for I *am* God, and *there is* none else; *I am* God, and *there is* none like me, declaring the end from the beginning, and from ancient times *the things* that are not *yet* done, saying, My counsel shall stand, and I will do all my pleasure." Isaiah 46:9, 10.

NOTE: *Through the prophetic gift God has predicted the course of world empires, the destiny of nations and cities, many events in the earthly life of Jesus, and numerous events and trends of these last days. Only God could predict so accurately events hundreds and thousands of years before they occurred.*

How does the Psalmist describe the eternal nature of God?

"Before the mountains were brought forth, or ever thou hadst formed the earth and the world, even from everlasting to everlasting, thou *art* God." Psalm 90:2.

In what language does the Bible tell us that God is every-where present?

"Whither shall I go from thy spirit? or whither shall I flee from thy presence? If I ascend up into heaven, thou *art* there: if I make my bed in hell, behold, thou *art there. If* I take the wings of the morning, *and* dwell in the uttermost parts of the sea; even there shall thy hand lead me, and thy right hand shall hold me. If I say, Surely the darkness shall cover me; even the night shall be light about me. Yea, the darkness hideth not from thee; but the night shineth as the day: the darkness and the light *are* both alike *to thee*." Psalm 139:7-12.

How did God describe His self-existent nature?

"And God said unto Moses, I AM THAT I AM: and he said, Thus shalt thou say unto the children of Israel, I AM hath sent me unto you." Exodus 3:14.

NOTE: *In Hebrew, as in English, this phrase "I AM" is a form of the verb "to be" and implies that its possessor is the eternal, self-existing One.*

God is all-powerful. "Almighty" is the the word used in the Bible. Is there anything beyond His capacity?

"And Jesus looking upon them saith, With men *it is* impossible, but not with God: for with God all things are possible." Mark 10:27.

How does the Bible indicate that, in form, man resembles his Maker?

"And God said, Let us make man in our image, after our likeness: and let them have dominion over the fish of the sea, and over the fowl of the air, and over the cattle, and over all the earth, and over every creeping thing that creepeth upon the earth." Genesis 1:26.

"And he said, Thou canst not see my face: for there shall no man see me, and live. And the Lord said, Behold, *there is* a place by me, and thou shalt stand upon a rock: And it shall come to pass, while my glory passeth by, that I will put thee in a clift of the rock, and will cover thee with my hand while I pass by: And I will take away mine hand, and thou shalt see my back parts: but my face shall not be seen." Exodus 33:20-23.

Due to our human limitations, what is it not possible for us to know about God?

"Canst thou by searching find out God? canst thou find out the Almighty unto perfection?" Job 11:7.

"Hast thou not known? hast thou not heard, *that* the everlasting God, the Lord, the Creator of the ends of the earth, fainteth not, neither is weary? *there is* no searching of his understanding." Isaiah 40:28.

NOTE: *No more can an ant fully know and understand man and his ways than can man know and fully understand all there is to know about God and His infinite wisdom, knowledge and power.*

How did God describe His loving and merciful character to Moses!

"And the Lord descended in the cloud, and stood with him there, and proclaimed the name of the Lord And the Lord passed by before him, and proclaimed, The Lord, The Lord God, merciful and gracious, long-suffering, and abundant in goodness and truth, keeping mercy for thousands, forgiving iniquity and transgression and sin, and that will by no means clear *the guilty;* visiting the iniquity of the fathers upon the children, and upon the children's children, unto the third and to the fourth *generation.*" Exodus 34:5-7.

To forever remove the misconception in human minds regarding God's true nature, how did the apostle John describe God?

"He that loveth not knoweth not God; for God is love." 1 John 4:8.

What supreme evidence has God given us of His love?

"For God so loved the world, that he gave his only begotten Son, that whosoever believeth in him should not perish, but have everlasting life." John 3:16.

The great God of the universe is our loving heavenly Father.

"'God is love' is written upon every opening bud, upon every spire of springing grass. The lovely birds making the air vocal with their happy songs, the delicately tinted flowers in their perfection perfuming the air, . . . testify to the . . . care of our God, and to His desire to make His children happy."—*Steps to Christ,* page 10.

When Philip said to Jesus, "Show us the Father," Jesus answered. "He that hath seen Me hath seen the Father." Jesus came not only to die for us, but to reveal God to us. He went about doing good, healing the sick, comforting the sorrowing, feeding the hungry, and forgiving penitents their sins. This was His character, and He and the Father are One, for Jesus was God "manifest in the flesh."

The cross of Christ is the fullest revelation of God's love, for "God was in Christ, reconciling the world unto Himself."

Like the father in the parable of the prodigal son, our heavenly Father opens wide His loving arms to each of us, His wayward children, and invites us to come to Him. The most wonderful thing you can do is to accept His invitation and come to know Him for yourself, for Jesus said, "This is life eternal, that they might know Thee the only true God, and Jesus Christ, whom Thou hast sent."

"All thy children shall be taught of the Lord; and great shall be the peace of thy children."

Isaiah 54:13

The Origin Of Evil

In a recent demonstration of remote control by the United States Air Force, a pilotless jet aircraft wheeled onto the runway of an airport, taxied to a predetermined spot, turned into the wind, and took off. The plane went through a number of maneuvers, circled the field several times, and made an almost perfect landing.

Those invited to view this demonstration looked on with admiration. Not one spectator thought that the plane was flying by itself. They knew that there was a master intelligence behind the maneuvers of that craft.

As one views the daily sinister events of death, terror, and violence reported by television, radio, and newspaper, it is evident that a master intelligence is operating in this world. He is at war, not only with God, but with all that is just and good.

While nations talk about peace, they prepare for war! While man plans for a world without crime, lawlessness skyrockets. While he searches for the means of stamping out death, new diseases and problems arise. More than one statesman has remarked, "There is something devilish at work in the world today."

In many circles today the devil has been voted out of existence. Many equate Satan with evil thoughts or a superstitious carry-over of a medieval fable. Christ and the prophets believed in the existence of an evil being. In the Bible he bears such names as the devil, Satan, the prince of this world, the deceiver, the serpent.

Where did the devil originate? Why hasn't God destroyed him? These and many other questions arise when he is mentioned. Let us turn to the Bible to learn the truth about Satan.

With whom did sin originate?

"He that committeth sin is of the devil; for the devil sinneth from the beginning. For this purpose the Son of God was manifested, that he might destroy the works of the devil." 1 John 3:8.

What kind of angel was Satan before his rebellion?

"Son of man, take up a lamentation upon the king of Tyrus, and say unto him, Thus saith the Lord God; Thou sealest up the sum, full of wisdom, and perfect in beauty." Ezekiel 28:12.

NOTE: *Under the figure of the king of Tyre, Ezekiel describes the activities of Lucifer. He was created "perfect," but he abused his power of choice. From an angel of light he turned himself into the devil by an act of his own will.*

What exalted position did Satan once occupy in the courts of heaven?

"Thou art the anointed cherub that covereth; and I have set thee so: thou wast upon the holy mountain of God; thou hast walked up and down in the midst of the stones of fire." Ezekiel 28:14.

NOTE: *As a covering cherub he stood next to God. Psalm 80:1.*

What higher position did this exalted being covet?

"How art thou fallen from heaven, O Lucifer, son of the morning! how art thou cut down to the ground, which didst weaken the nations! For thou hast said in thine heart, I will ascend into heaven, I will exalt my throne above the stars of God: I will sit also upon the mount of the congregation, in the sides of the north: I will ascend above the heights of the clouds; I will be like the Most High." Isaiah 14:12-14.

NOTE: *Another motive behind his rebellion was pride of his beauty. Ezekiel 28:17.*

What did God do when Satan's rebellion led to war in heaven?

"And there was war in heaven: Michael and his angels fought against the dragon; and the dragon fought and his angels, and prevailed not; neither was their place found any more in heaven. And the great dragon was cast out, that old serpent, called the Devil, and Satan, which deceiveth the whole world: he was cast out into the earth, and his angels were cast out with him." Revelation 12:7-9.

When he was cast out of heaven, whom did Satan then seek to deceive?

"Now the serpent was more subtil than any beast of the field which the Lord had made. And he said unto the woman, Yea, hath God said, Ye shall not eat of every tree of the garden? And the woman said unto the serpent, We may eat of the fruit of the trees of the garden: but of the fruit of the tree which *is* in the midst of the garden, God hath said, Ye shall not eat of it, neither shall ye touch it, lest ye die. And the serpent said unto the woman, Ye shall not surely die: For God doth know that in the day ye eat thereof, then your eyes shall be opened, and ye shall be as gods, knowing good and evil. And when the woman saw that the tree was good for food, and that it was pleasant to the eyes, and a tree to be desired to make *one* wise, she took of the fruit thereof, and did eat, and gave also unto her husband with her; and he did eat." Genesis 3:1-6.

NOTE: Satan used the serpent as a medium to attract the attention of the woman.

What does Satan now claim as his?

"And the devil, taking him up into an high mountain, shewed unto him all the kingdoms of the world in a moment of time. And the devil said unto him, All this power will I give thee, and the glory of them: for that is delivered unto me; and to whomsoever I will give it." Luke 4:5, 6.

NOTE: See also Job 1:6-8. Satan appeared at the gates of heaven claiming to be the representative of this world. The "sons of God" mentioned in these verses were the unfallen representatives of other worlds.

Who brings sickness and trouble upon mankind?

"So went Satan forth from the presence of the Lord, and smote Job with sore boils from the sole of his foot unto his crown." Job 2:7.

"And ought not this woman, being a daughter of Abraham, whom Satan hath bound, lo, these eighteen years, be loosed from this bond on the sabbath day?" Luke 13:16.

How will this evil one finally be destroyed by God?

"By the multitude of thy merchandise they have filled the midst of thee with violence, and thou hast sinned: therefore I will cast thee as profane out of the mountain of God: and I will destroy thee, O covering cherub, from the midst of the stones of fire. Thine heart was lifted up because of thy beauty, thou hast corrupted thy wisdom by reason of thy brightness: I will cast thee to the ground, I will lay thee before kings, that they may behold thee. Thou hast defiled thy sanctuaries by the multitude of thine iniquities, by the iniquity of thy traffick; therefore will I bring forth a fire from the midst of thee, it shall devour thee, and I will bring thee to ashes upon the earth in the sight of all them that behold thee. All they that know thee among the people shall be astonished at thee: thou shalt be a terror, and never *shalt* thou *be* any more." Ezekiel 28:16-19.

Why does the devil work so viciously now?

"And I heard a loud voice saying in heaven, Now is come salvation, and strength, and the kingdom of our God, and the power of his Christ: for the accuser of our brethren is cast down, which accused them before our God day and night. . . . Therefore rejoice, *ye* heavens, and ye that dwell in them. Woe to the inhabiters of the earth and of the sea! for the devil is come down unto you, having great wrath, because he knoweth that he hath but a short time." Revelation 12: 10, 12.

How does Satan seek to disguise himself and his activities?

"For such *are* false prophets, deceitful workers, transforming themselves into the apostles of Christ. And no marvel; for Satan himself is transformed into an angel of light. Therefore *it is* no great thing if his ministers also be transformed as the ministers of righteousness; whose end shall be according to their works." 2 Corinthians 11:13-15.

What is man's only defense against the devil's deceptions?

"Put on the whole armour of God, that ye may be able to stand against the wiles of the devil. For we wrestle not against flesh and blood, but against principalities, against powers, against the rulers of the darkness of this world, against spiritual wickedness in high *places*." Ephesians 6:11, 12.

How can we gain victory over this archenemy?

"And they overcame him by the blood of the Lamb, and by the word of their testimony; and they loved not their lives unto the death." Revelation 12:11.

Peter warns us, "Your adversary the devil, as a roaring lion, walketh about, seeking whom he may devour." 1 Peter 5:8. Never have his deceptions been so effective in misleading and destroying men as they are today. He especially directs his anger against those who are loyal to God.

The devil sought to overcome the Saviour before He could accomplish His mission of redemption. Christ was victorious in every battle fought with the deceiver. The Bible tells us that Christ did not sin. By His death on the cross of Calvary He earned the right to deliver those held in bondage by Satan if they will accept His death in their stead. By instigating Christ's death, the devil signed his own death decree.

Satan will soon be destroyed with all those who have yielded to his temptations to sin. The Bible assures us that his end will be complete. But now he seeks to deceive even the children of God. The same Redeemer who gained the complete victory in His battle with Satan is able to give you the victory too if you will place your life in His hands—hands that were pierced for your sins. Trust Him this day, and He will give you forgiveness for past sins and victory over future temptations.

All sin is a manifestation of selfishness in some form, and its results are the opposite of those prompted by love.

"What Think Ye Of Christ?"

Following World War II a Christian worker was making his way through the debris-choked streets of Berlin. Seeing a young man, he asked, "Young man, do you know Jesus Christ?" The young man looked perplexed and answered, "No, sir, I'm not acquainted with Him. You might ask at the local police station. Perhaps they know where He lives."

There are millions of people in this country who, though having a faint knowledge of the historical facts surrounding the life of Jesus Christ, really do not know Him. From the pulpits of many churches today we are told that Jesus was a great teacher, that He was a great preacher, or that He was a great social reformer. Christ has become nothing more than a great humanitarian to many who call themselves Christians today. They have rejected His miraculous birth, death, and resurrection.

Someone may ask, "What difference does it make what I believe about Jesus Christ as long as I believe that He lived and that He died 1,900 years ago?" What you believe about Jesus Christ, His origin, His life, His death, and His present mission will make all the difference in the world to your salvation and your relationship to God. Either Christ was what He claimed to be, the Saviour of mankind who died to deliver us from our sins, or He was the greatest impostor the world has ever known. The transformations which take place in the lives of those who fully accept Him demonstrate that He is a wonderful Saviour.

In a prophecy connected with the birth of Christ, how long does it say that He has existed?

"But thou, Bethlehem Ephratah, *though* thou be little among the thousands of Judah, *yet* out of thee shall he come forth unto me *that is* to be ruler in Israel; whose goings forth *have been* from of old, from everlasting." Micah 5:2.

How long did Jesus say He had been with God the Father?

"And now, O Father, glorify thou me with thine own self with the glory which I had with thee before the world was." John 17:5.

What does God the Father call the Son?

"But unto the Son *he saith,* Thy throne, O God, *is* for ever and ever: a sceptre of righteousness *is* the sceptre of thy kingdom." Hebrews 1:8.

What fulness dwells in Christ?

"For in him dwelleth all the fulness of the Godhead bodily." Colossians 2:9.

In accepting Christ as His Saviour, how did Thomas address Him?

"And Thomas answered and said unto him, My Lord and my God." John 20:28.

Using the term "the Word," what does John state that Christ was?

"In the beginning was the Word, and the Word was with God, and the Word was God." John 1:1.

"And the Word was made flesh, and dwelt among us, (and we beheld his glory, the glory as of the only begotten of the Father,) full of grace and truth." John 1:14.

NOTE: The Greek word translated "the Word" means the thought of God expressed. That is Jesus was the revelation of God's character, mind, and will. Some teach that Jesus was "a god." But that is definitely not what John said. He said that from the very beginning the Word, or Jesus, was God, not one among many, but God essentially.

Who created the world?

"In the beginning was the Word, and the Word was with God, and the Word was God. The same was in the beginning with God. All things were made by him; and without him was not any thing made that was made. . . . And the Word was made flesh, and dwelt among us, (and we beheld his glory, the glory as of the only begotten of the Father,) full of grace and truth." John 1:1-3, 14.

How many things were created by Jesus Christ?

"Who is the image of the invisible God, the firstborn of every creature: For by him were all things created, that are in heaven, and that are in earth, visible and invisible, whether *they be* thrones, or dominions, or principalities, or powers: all things were created by him, and for him: And he is before all things, and by him all things consist." Colossians 1:15-17.

How does Christ describe the unity that exists between Him and the Father?

"I and *my* Father are one." John 10:30.

At the baptism of Christ, what did the Father call Jesus?

"And Jesus, when he was baptized, went up straightway out of the water: and, lo, the heavens were opened unto him, and he saw the Spirit of God descending like a dove, and lighting upon him: And lo a voice from heaven, saying, This is my beloved Son, in whom I am well pleased." Matthew 3:16, 17.

NOTE: Three Persons comprise the Godhead—the Father, the Son, and the Holy Spirit. See Matthew 28:19. Three Persons, but one God. This is a mystery beyond human comprehension.

By what miracle was Christ born into this world?

"Now the birth of Jesus Christ was on this wise: When as his mother Mary was espoused to Joseph, before they came together, she was found with child of the Holy Ghost . . . But while he thought on these things, behold, the angel of the Lord appeared unto him in a dream, saying, Joseph, thou son of David, fear not to take unto thee Mary thy wife: for that which is conceived in her is of the Holy Ghost." Matthew 1:18, 20.

"And the angel answered and said unto her, The Holy Ghost shall come upon thee, and the power of the Highest shall overshadow thee: therefore also that Holy thing which shall be born of thee shall be called the Son of God." Luke 1:35.

For what purpose did Christ come to this world?

"And she shall bring forth a son, and thou shalt call his name JESUS: for he shall save his people from their sins." Matthew 1:21.

What type of life did Christ live?

"For even hereunto were ye called: because Christ also suffered for us, leaving us an example, that ye should follow his steps: Who did no sin, neither was guile found in his mouth." 1 Peter 2:21, 22.

How did Christ pay the penalty for our sins that we might be forgiven?

"Who, when he was reviled, reviled not again; when he suffered, he threatened not; but committed *himself* to him that judgeth righteously: Who his own self bare our sins in his own body on the tree, that we, being dead to sins, should live unto righteousness: by whose stripes ye were healed." 1 Peter 2:23, 24.

What wonderful transaction takes place when we accept Christ as our Saviour from sin?

"To wit, that God was in Christ, reconciling the world unto himself, not imputing their trespasses unto them; and hath committed unto us the word of reconciliation. Now then we are ambassadors for Christ, as though God did beseech *you* by us: we pray *you* in Christ's stead, be ye reconciled to God. For he hath made him *to be* sin for us, who knew no sin; that we might be made the righteousness of God in him." 2 Corinthians 5:19-21.

How only may we receive eternal life?

"For God so loved the world, that he gave his only begotten Son, that whosoever believeth in him should not perish, but have everlasting life." John 3:16.

By accepting Christ and His sacrifice, what will we receive?

"And this is the record, that God hath given to us eternal life, and this life is in his Son. He that hath the Son hath life; and he that hath not the Son of God hath not life." 1 John 5:11, 12.

After Christ had spent some time with His disciples, He asked them the searching question, "Whom do men say that I the Son of Man am?" Various answers were given by them. Some said that Christ was John the Baptist. Others said that He was Elijah. And still others thought He was one of the great prophets. The Jewish people were looking for a mighty king to come as the Messiah to deliver them from Roman bondage. They were more concerned with their political condition than they were with spiritual deliverance from their sins. Consequently, when Christ made His appearance as a humble Teacher from Nazareth, most of the people were unwilling to accept Him as the Messiah.

Today, many are like the people of Christ's time. They are looking for some mighty leader to solve the problems of modern society, atomic warfare, disease and sickness. These things seem more important than the matter of salvation from sin. After Christ had received the various answers from the disciples, He said to them, "But whom say ye that I am? And Simon Peter answered and said, Thou art the Christ, the Son of the living God." Matthew 16:15, 16.

Christ commended Peter for his statement and indicated that this truth had been revealed to him by God. Upon this foundation the Christian church was to be established and built. Jesus Christ is indeed the divine Son of God. He came from heaven to reveal God's love to man and to demonstrate by His death upon the cross of Calvary how much God loves His wayward children. Jesus also loves us, for He gave Himself for us.

As we view the dying Saviour upon the cross of Calvary, our hearts respond in deepest gratitude and love. We can do no less than give our sinful lives and hearts to Him to wash away our sins and prepare us to live with Him throughout eternity.

It is a great privilege to join Peter in his declaration and Thomas in his acceptance of Christ as Lord and God.

"He that hath the Son hath life; and he that hath not the Son of God hath not life."

1 John 5:12

The Problem Of Sin

Some time ago the newspapers carried a story of a little girl who had been playing in the garage of her home when she found a bottle full of what looked like soft drink that her mother at times gave her. She turned the bottle up and drank the fluid in it, even though it tasted strange. Soon she began to experience pains in her stomach. When she complained to her mother, she was rushed to the hospital for treatment. Sad to say, help came too late, and the little girl paid with her life for her experiment with that strange substance in the bottle. What she thought was a soft drink actually was a weed killer, deadly to human beings.

Sin is as deadly to the soul as weed killer is to the body. Many people today do not realize that they are poisoned with sin and will die from this killer. We have seen in the study of a previous lesson how Satan works to deceive and destroy all of God's children that he possibly can.

We may have had friends who died from cancer who could have been cured if the cancer had been detected sooner to permit early treatment. They didn't know what was wrong until it was too late. Just so, many who are diseased with sin do not recognize their lost condition. They congratulate themselves on their good works and may say, "Surely the Lord would not refuse to save a person as good as I am." The Lord is anxious to save all that He can, but He cannot save any one of us unless we recognize our sinfulness and come to Him for forgiveness and salvation. Paul became a great Christian because he realized that he was a great sinner and went to God for cleansing. We need to know what sin is so that we will not be deceived by it. Then we need to acknowledge our true condition and receive help from God.

What does God say that sin is?

"Whosoever committeth sin transgresseth also the law: for sin is the transgression of the law." 1 John 3:4.

What command convinced Paul that he was a sinner?

"What shall we say then? *Is* the law sin? God forbid. Nay, I had not known sin, but by the law: for I had not known lust except the law had said, Thou shalt not covet." Romans 7:7.

NOTE: *Paul here quotes the tenth of the Ten Commandments. He shows that he thought that he was without sin until the law showed him that he was a transgressor of the tenth commandment.*

By what law will God judge us to see whether or not we are sinners?

"For whosoever shall keep the whole law, and yet offend in one *point*, he is guilty of all. For he that said, Do not commit adultery, said also, Do not kill. Now if thou commit no adultery, yet if thou kill, thou art become a transgressor of the law. So speak ye, and so do, as they that shall be judged by the law of liberty." James 2:10-12.

NOTE: Here again James quotes from the Ten Commandments in showing what sin is.

What does the first commandment prohibit?

"Thou shalt have no other gods before me." Exodus 20:3.

NOTE: If we worship other gods we are sinners.

What objects did God forbid His people to worship?

"Thou shalt not make unto thee any graven image, or any likeness of *any* thing that is in heaven above, or that is in the earth beneath, or that is in the water under the earth: Thou shalt not bow down thyself to them, nor serve them: for I the Lord thy God *am* a jealous God, visiting the iniquity of the fathers upon the children unto the third and fourth *generation* of them that hate me, and shewing mercy unto thousands of them that love me, and keep my commandments." Exodus 20:4-6.

NOTE: This command prohibits the worship of any thing.

What command shows God's disapproval of disrespectful speech?

"Thou shalt not take the name of the Lord thy God in vain; for the Lord will not hold him guiltless that taketh his name in vain." Exodus 20:7.

What does God instruct us to remember?

"Remember the sabbath day, to keep it holy." Exodus 20:8.

What does God indicate should be our relationship to our parents?

"Honour thy father and thy mother: that thy days may be long upon the land which the Lord thy God giveth thee." Exodus 20:12.

What command forbids murder?

"Thou shalt not kill." Exodus 20:13.

NOTE: Christ pointed out that intense hatred within the heart is violation of this command Matthew 5:21, 22.

What does God command in respect to immorality?

"Thou shalt not commit adultery." Exodus 20:14.

NOTE: Jesus interpreted this commandment in Matthew 5:27, 28.

What did God say to show that taking the property of others is wrong?

"Thou shalt not steal." Exodus 20:15.

How does God show the sinfulness of being untruthful?

"Thou shalt not bear false witness against thy neighbour." Exodus 20:16.

NOTE: Liars will be outside the New Jerusalem Revelation 21:27.

What command forbids greed?

"Thou shalt not covet thy neighbour's house, thou shalt not covet thy neighbour's wife, nor his manservant, nor his maidservant, nor his ox, nor his ass, nor anything that is thy neighbour's." Exodus 20:17.

NOTE: *This is the last of the Ten Commandments. In these ten simple rules God gives us a measuring rod by which we can tell right from wrong in our relationship to both God and our fellowmen. These ten commands of God cover every sin that men commit.*

How inclusive does God make the definition of sin?

"All unrighteousness is sin: and there is a sin not unto death." 1 John 5:17.

NOTE: *Every wrong act, every act of rebellion against God, is sin. Every unrighteous thought or act is an evidence that we are sinners in need of God's saving grace.*

According to the Bible how many of us have broken God's commandments and sinned?

"Wherefore, as by one man sin entered into the world, and death by sin; and so death passed upon all men, for that all have sinned." Romans 5:12.

What fact gives the sinner hope of salvation from sin?

"This *is* a faithful saying, and worthy of all acceptation, that Christ Jesus came into the world to save sinners; of whom I am chief." 1 Timothy 1:15.

The Bible tells us that God is not willing that any should perish. 2 Peter 3:9. The loving Father longs to see each sinner saved from sin and death. To prove this beyond doubt He gave His only-begotten Son, Jesus, to die for our salvation on the cross of Calvary. However, God will not force the sinner to accept cleansing and salvation. It is only when we as sinners recognize our true condition and come to God with a deep sense of our own need that He is able to forgive and save us. Christ illustrated this truth beautifully in the story of the Pharisee and the publican. He said, "Two men went up into the temple to pray; the one a Pharisee, and the other a publican. The Pharisee stood and prayed thus with himself, God, I thank Thee, that I am not as other men are, extortioners, unjust, adulterers, or even as this publican, standing afar off, would not lift up so much as his eyes unto heaven, but smote upon his breast, saying, God be merciful to me a sinner. I tell you, this man went down to his house justified rather than the other." Luke 18:10-14.

As far as society was concerned the Pharisee was an "ideal" citizen and the publican was far from what he should have been. The publican, however, recognized his need of a change and forgiveness. The Pharisee felt no need of God's help and therefore he received no forgiveness. He went down to his house unjustified, unforgiven. The publican, on the other hand, felt his great need and prayed to the loving heavenly Father, who readily forgave him for his past sins.

If you feel like the publican as you view your past mistakes and sins, if you recognize as you have studied this lesson that you have disobeyed God and lived contrary to His Word, why not acknowledge your sins and find forgiveness and freedom from sin by accepting God's offer to save you today?

Sin And Its Cure

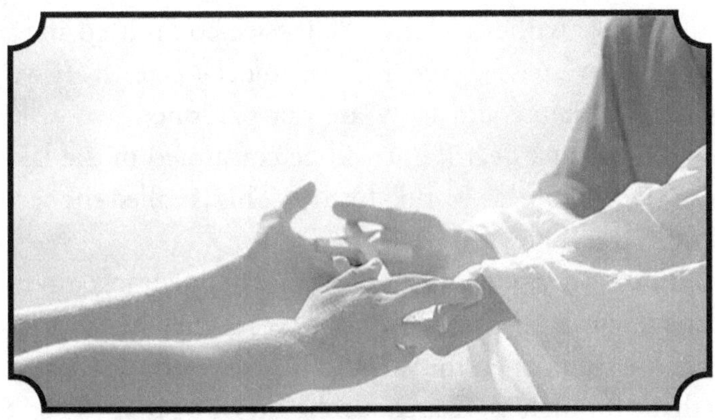

A number of years ago, a young man, Carol Chessman, was convicted of kidnapping and sentenced to die in the death chamber. Naturally, he did not want to die. For years he waged a stubborn fight for his life.

He secured a number of law books and studied as he had never studied before. His very life depended upon his ability to find some way to escape the death penalty, or at least delay execution of the death sentence.

One legal maneuver after another was tried by this man, postponing the fearful day when he would lose his life. For months and years he was able to stall for time. During this period of waiting he even had time to write a book telling his story and the reason why he thought he should be released. Finally the appeal was made and turned down. His last chance of pardon had been exhausted. There was no more hope! Down to the last minute he held onto a thread of hope that he would be saved. But that failed and he was executed. The courts had found him guilty and now the state carried out the sentence.

As we think of this man desperately fighting for every hour that could lengthen his life, it reminds us of the plight of the sinner without Christ. When we committed the first wrong act, we passed under the sentence of death. If we do not receive mercy and if we are not pardoned, we will not only die the first death, but will be consumed in the lake of fire at the end of this world's history. This is called the second death in the Bible.

Life is very precious and a man will do almost anything to try to prolong these few short years that he is granted. When we think of eternity, without pain, sorrow, sickness, or death, how much more anxious should we be to make certain we do not lose eternal life. If every person were as earnest in seeking eternal life as Mr. Chessman was in prolonging his life on this earth, there would be far more people saved when Christ returns.

What is sin?

"Whosoever committeth sin transgresseth also the law: for sin is the transgression of the law." 1 John 3:4.

NOTE: *All unrighteousness is sin. Every act of rebellion against God and His way of life is sin.*

How many of the human race have sinned?

"As it is written, There is none righteous, no, not one." Romans 3:10.

"For all have sinned, and come short of the glory of God." Romans 3:23.

What has been the result of the entrance of sin into this world?

"Wherefore, as by one man sin entered into the world, and death by sin; and so death passed upon all men, for that all have sinned." Romans 5:12.

What are the wages of sin?

"For the wages of sin is death; but the gift of God is eternal life through Jesus Christ our Lord." Romans 6:23.

"And death and hell were cast into the lake of fire. This is the second death. And whosoever was not found written in the book of life was cast into the lake of fire." Revelation 20:14, 15.

What does God promise to give us through Jesus Christ?

"For the wages of sin is death; but the gift of God is eternal life through Jesus Christ our Lord." Romans 6:23.

Through what means does God intend to take away our sins?

"The next day John seeth Jesus coming unto him, and saith, Behold the Lamb of God, which taketh away the sin of the world." John 1:29.

How does the Lamb of God cleanse us from all sin?

"For when we were yet without strength, in due time Christ died for the ungodly. For scarcely for a righteous man will one die: yet peradventure for a good man some would even dare to die. But God commendeth his love toward us, in that, while we were yet sinners, Christ died for us. Much more then, being now justified by his blood, we shall be saved from wrath through him." Romans 5:6-9.

What is the cleansing agent used by God to make us clean?

"But if we walk in the light, as he is in the light, we have fellowship one with another, and the blood of Jesus Christ his Son cleanseth us from all sin." 1 John 1:7.

When we fully realize that it was for our sins that Christ died, what will we want to know?

"Therefore let all the house of Israel know assuredly, that God hath made that same Jesus, whom ye have crucified, both Lord and Christ. Now when they heard *this*, they were pricked in their heart, and said unto Peter and to the rest of the apostles, Men *and* brethren, what shall we do?" Acts 2:36, 37.

What must we do before God can cleanse us from sin?

"Repent ye therefore, and be converted, that your sins may be blotted out, when the times of refreshing shall come from the presence of the Lord." Acts 3:19.

"Then Peter said unto them, Repent, and be baptized every one of you in the name of Jesus Christ for the remission of sins, and ye shall receive the gift of the Holy Ghost." Acts 2:38.

True repentance will lead us to do what two things?

"He that covereth his sins shall not prosper: but whoso confesseth and forsaketh *them* shall have mercy." Proverbs 28:13.

If we confess our sins and ask for forgiveness what does God promise to do?

"If we confess our sins, he is faithful and just to forgive us *our* sins, and to cleanse us from all unrighteousness." 1 John 1:9.

How complete will be the forgiveness that God promises to the penitent?

"For I will be merciful to their unrighteousness, and their iniquities will I remember no more." Hebrews 8:12.

How unworthy did Paul feel in his sinful state?

"This is a faithful saying, and worthy of all acceptation, that Christ Jesus came into the world to save sinners; of whom I am chief." 1 Timothy 1:15.

What assurance filled Paul's heart as he neared the end of his life?

"I have fought a good fight, I have finished *my* course, I have kept the faith. Henceforth there is laid up for me a crown of righteousness, which the Lord the righteous judge, shall give me at that day: and not to me only, but unto all them also that love his appearing." 2 Timothy 4:7, 8.

How did Paul tell the jailer that he could receive salvation?

"And they said, Believe on the Lord Jesus Christ, and thou shalt be saved, and thy house." Acts 16:31.

Paul became a great saint because he first recognized that he was a great sinner. He went to the One who could so change him to become like his Master. At the time of his conversion he was on the way to Damascus to kill the Christians there. He thought he had been doing the will of God, but soon realized that he had been doing the work of the enemy. When he was shown his error, he was willing to let God change him. He made a complete surrender of self. He was willing to let God show him the way that he should go. Like Paul, we must recognize our sinfulness and repent of our sins. When we realize that it was those sins that broke the heart of our Saviour and caused His death upon the Cross of Calvary, we will come to Him for cleansing and His blood will make us white as snow.

If you feel your need of forgiveness, why not come to Christ this very day? Confess your sins and let God lift the load of guilt and shame. He will freely forgive and forget your sins. He invites you to come. "Come now and let us reason together, saith the Lord: though your sins be as scarlet, they shall be as white as snow, though they be red like crimson, they shall be as wool." Isaiah 1:18.

A simple, sincere prayer, offered from a heart burdened with guilt, will bring freedom from the sense of that guilt. One of the most eloquent prayers ever offered was given by a 78-year-old man. He simply prayed, "Dear Lord, be merciful and forgive all of my sins and I will be much obliged to you. Amen." He found forgiveness through Christ. We can be certain that God heard and answered that prayer, for it came from the depth of his heart. Won't you reach out and receive Christ as your Saviour today and be certain of complete forgiveness? As you see the door of mercy opening to you, make your decision today.

How You Can Become
A New Person

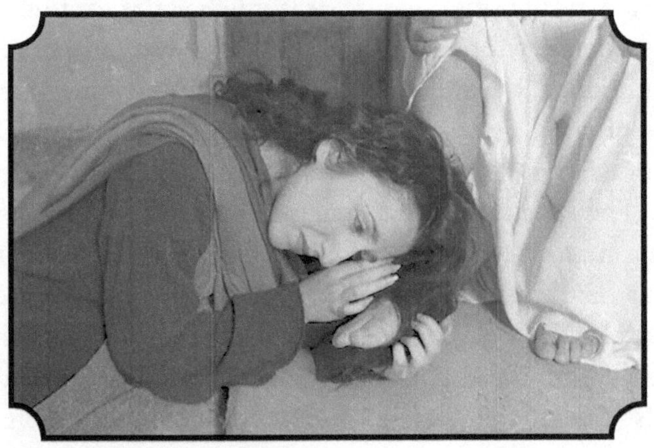

Some time ago the newspapers told the story of a young girl who had raised a panther as a pet. It was only a few days old when it was given to her. The girl was ever so kind to this pet and the two of them spent many hours together in play.

As the panther grew larger and older, the girl was warned of the danger of having this wild animal for a pet. She had almost grown up with the panther and was certain that the animal would never harm her. She claimed that all the wild traits of this particular cat had been eliminated by its constant association with humans.

Then one day the girl cut her finger as she was playing with the animal. The panther licked the blood from the wound. In a matter of a few seconds this kind, gentle play-mate became a ravenous beast. Knocking its master to the ground it viciously chewed and clawed her. The girl was certain the nature of the panther had been changed by its association with humans, but she discovered that it still had the nature and heart of a wild animal.

This story illustrates the nature of man. Man is born with a basically sinful nature. It is much easier for him to do that which is wrong and sinful than that which is good and right. Education and training may develop some outward signs of good behaviour, but the evil nature inherited from Adam will remain.

The kind father and thoughtful husband can become a raging maniac when he has had a few drinks. Psychologists tell us that these outbreaks are due to hidden and repressed drives that are held in check by self control but show themselves when the self control is temporarily anesthetized. Christ said that the religious leaders of His day were like "whited sepulchres, which indeed appear beautiful outward, but are within full of dead men's bones and of all uncleanness." Matthew 23:27.

In order to be right with God we need forgiveness for our past sins. More than this, we need the evil nature, which produces these sins, changed.

What does the Bible say it is impossible for the sinner to do?
"Can the Ethiopian change his skin, or the leopard his spots? *then* may ye also do good, that are accustomed to do evil." Jeremiah 13:23.

How does Isaiah describe the good deeds we are capable of doing?

"But we are all as unclean *thing*, and all our righteousness *are* as rags; and we all do fade as a leaf; and our iniquities, like the wind, have taken us away." Isaiah 64:6.

When Paul wanted to do that which was right, what did he do instead?

"For that which I do I allow not: for what I would, that do I not; but what I hate, that do I. If then I do that which I would not, I consent unto the law that *it is* good. Now then it is no more I that do it, but sin that dwelleth in me. For I know that in me (that is, in my flesh,) dwelleth no good thing: for to will is present with me; but *how* to perform that which is good I find not. For the good that I would I do not: but the evil which I would not, that I do." Romans 7:15-19.

Why was Paul incapable of doing what God commanded?

"For we know that the law is spiritual; but I am carnal, sold under sin." Romans 7:14.

What does the Bible say is the reason that mankind does not willingly obey God?

"For to be carnally minded *is* death; but to be spiritually minded *is* life and peace. Because the carnal mind *is* enmity against God: for it is not subject to the law of God, neither indeed can be." Romans 8:6, 7.

How can a lost sinner become a child of God?

"Repent ye therefore, and be converted, that your sins may be blotted out, when the times of refreshing shall come from the presence of the Lord." Acts 3:19.

NOTE: *This text tells us to repent and be converted. The word converted means to be changed. We are to have the carnal nature changed into spiritual nature. Our part is to repent or be sorry for our sins. God's part is to accomplish the change in us which we call conversion.*

How can our natures be changed from carnal to spiritual so that we might be what God wants us to be?

"Jesus answered, Verily, verily, I say unto thee, Except a man be born again, he cannot see the kingdom of God." John 3:3.

How does God accomplish this spiritual rebirth?

"Jesus answered, Verily, verily, I say unto thee, Except a man be born of water and *of* the Spirit, he cannot enter into the kingdom of God. That which is born of the flesh is flesh; and that which is born of the Spirit is spirit." John 3:5, 6.

"But as many as received him, to them gave he power to become the sons of God, even to them that believe on his name: which were born, not of blood, nor of the will of the flesh, nor of the will of man, but of God." John 1:12, 13.

What does God promise to do if we yield ourselves to Him?

"A new heart also will I give you, and a new spirit will I put within you: and I will take away the stony heart out of your flesh, and I will give you an heart of flesh." Ezekiel 36:26.

Under the new covenant what has God promised to do to help us in living a Christian life?

"For this *is* the covenant that I will make with the house of Israel after those days, saith the Lord; I will put my laws into their mind, and write them in their hearts: and I will be to them a God, and they shall be to me a people." Hebrews 8:10.

Through whom does deliverance from the evil nature come?

"O wretched man that I am! who shall deliver me from the body of this death? I thank God through Jesus Christ our Lord. So then with the mind I myself serve the law of God; but with the flesh the law of sin." Romans 7:24, 25.

How deep must be our desire to receive this change?

"Blessed are they which do hunger and thirst after righteousness: for they shall be filled." Matthew 5:6.

When will we be able to find the help we need in securing salvation?

"Then shall ye call upon me, and ye shall go and pray unto me, and I will hearken unto you. And ye shall seek me, and find *me*, when ye shall search for me with all your heart." Jeremiah 29:12, 13.

How completely are we changed by this rebirth through Christ?

"Therefore if any man *be* in Christ, *he is* a new creature: old things are passed away; behold, all things are become new." 2 Corinthians 5:17.

How does the Bible describe the change that takes place by the new birth?

"If ye then be risen with Christ, seek those things which are above, where Christ sitteth on the right hand of God. Set your affection on things above, not on things on the earth. For ye are dead, and your life is hid with Christ in God.

When Christ, *who is* our life, shall appear, then shall ye also appear with him in glory. Mortify therefore your members which are upon the earth; fornication, uncleanness, inordinate affection, evil concupiscence, and covetousness, which is idolatry: For which things' sake the wrath of God cometh on the children of disobedience: In the which ye also walked some time, when ye lived in them. But now ye also put off all these; anger, wrath, malice, blasphemy, filthy communication out of your mouth. Lie not one to another, seeing that ye have put off the old man with his deeds; And have put on the new *man*, which is renewed in knowledge after the image of him that created him." Colossians 3:1-10.

When an individual has been truly converted, what new traits of character will be seen in his life?

"But the fruit of the Spirit is love, joy, peace, longsuffering, gentleness, goodness, faith, meekness, temperance: against such there is no law. And they that are Christ's have crucified the flesh with the affection and lusts. If we live in the Spirit, let us also walk in the Spirit." Galatians 5:22-25.

What assurance is given to those who are born of God?

"For whatsoever is born of God overcometh the world: and this is the victory that overcometh the world, *even* our faith." 1 John 5:4.

How many times each of us had failed in following the Saviour as he should. Many of us have tried so very hard to do right—only to fall more miserably than before. Our intentions were good, but we were trying to do good without God's help. We were still carnal and sinful in nature. We were controlled by passions and habits acquired before we knew God's plan of redemption. Without Jesus our hearts cannot be changed. We can never overcome the Devil in our own strength.

It is only as we put our lives in the hands of Christ that we can gain the victory over sins. It is only through Him that we can live the victorious Christian life.

So many have said, "When I overcome this habit, or gain the victory over that sin, then I will accept the Lord and become a Christian." This is like the sick person saying, "When I get well I will go to the doctor and let him help me." The time to come to Christ for help is when you recognize your need. Give Him your heart today and know the joy and peace that comes to you as you become a new creature in Christ. You can do this by dropping to your knees just now and letting Him take control of your life. Perhaps you do not know how to come to Christ. Just repeat these simple words as an expression of your heart's sincere desire: "Dear Lord, I am weak. I have sinned. Please forgive and help me. Come into my heart and change me just now. Amen."

"And every man that hath this hope in him purifieth himself, even as He is pure."

1 John 3:3

The Law And The Gospel

THE TEN COMMANDMENTS
AS ORIGINALLY GIVEN BY GOD
(Exodus 20:3-17)

I
Thou shalt have no other gods before Me.

II
Thou shalt not make unto thee any graven image, or any likeness of anything that is in heaven above, or that is in the earth beneath, or that is in the water under the earth: thou shalt not bow down thyself to them, nor serve them: for I the Lord thy God am a jealous God, visiting the iniquity of the fathers upon the children unto the third and fourth generation of them that hate Me; and showing mercy unto thousands of them that love Me, and keep My commandments.

III
Thou shalt not take the name of the Lord thy God in vain; for the Lord will not hold him guiltless that taketh His name in vain.

IV
Remember the Sabbath day, to keep it holy. Six days shalt thou labour, and do all thy work: but the seventh day is the Sabbath of the Lord thy God: in it thou shalt not do any work, thou, nor thy son, nor thy daughter, thy manservant, nor thy maidservant, nor the cattle, nor thy stranger that is within thy gates: for in six days the Lord made heaven and earth, the sea, and all that in them is, and rested the seventh day: wherefore the Lord blessed the Sabbath day, and hallowed it.

V
Honour thy father and thy mother: that thy days may be long upon the land which the Lord thy God giveth thee.

VI
Thou shalt not kill.

VII
Thou shalt not commit adultery.

VIII
Thou shalt not steal.

IX
Thou shalt not bear false witness against thy neighbour.

X
Thou shalt not covet thy neighbour's house, thou shalt not covet thy neighbour's wife, nor his manservant, nor his maidservant, nor his ox, nor his ass, nor anything that is thy neighbour's.

A certain man was locked in prison for breaking the law of the state. The judge sentenced him to several years of hard labor under the custody and supervision of trusted guards. After he had served two years a friend of the prisoner called upon the Governor. This friend convinced the Governor that the young prisoner should be pardoned and set free. "And," said the Governor, "I would like for you to take this letter of pardon to this lucky criminal."

With the pardon in his pocket, the prisoner's friend was admitted through the sturdy gates and doors of the prison. In a few moments this prisoner could be made free, and leave his hard labor and confinement. However, before handing him the Governor's pardon, this kind friend began to talk with his convict acquaintance who was suffering the penalty of the law. Finally the friend said, "If the Governor pardoned your crime and set you free, what would you do?"

"If I ever get out of this prison," retorted the young convict, "the first thing I am going to do is to buy a gun, and kill the old man who testified against me at my trial."

Sorrowfully the friend told the prisoner good-bye with the pardon still in his pocket. Then he returned the undelivered pardon to the Governor saying that the prisoner was not worthy of pardon.

Pardon from man or forgiveness of God is not freedom to break either human or divine laws. Today world leaders say that lawlessness is multiplying so rapidly that law enforcing agencies are unable to control it.

People in every nation are gravely concerned with the mounting disregard shown for the laws of the land. Many youth of today, after breaking the law of God and the law of the land, are increasingly rebellious. They are eager to commit greater and more horrible crimes. "We will set up our own standards," they declare. They are searching for happiness in a new freedom, freedom from law and order.

God has given men a moral standard to guide all of his actions. But men have ignored God's law and the world is in a chaos of lawlessness. The wanted happiness has not come.

God has not changed. The law of God, His moral standard, has not changed. Though men have ignored His law, it still stands. It is as up-to-date today as when it came from His hand. The Bible says, "He that keepeth the law, happy is he."

How does the Bible describe God's law?

"The law of the Lord *is* perfect, converting the soul: the testimony of the Lord *is* sure, making wise the simple." Psalm 19:7.

"Wherefore the law *is* holy, and the commandment holy, and just, and good." Romans 7:12.

What is one of the main purposes of the law?

"Now we know that what things soever the law saith, it saith to them who are under the law: that every mouth may be stopped, and all the world may become guilty before God. Therefore by the deeds of the law there shall no flesh be justified in his sight: for by the law *is* the knowledge of sin." Romans 3:19, 20.

What helped Paul to recognize sin in his life?

"What shall we say then? *Is* the law sin? God forbid. Nay, I had not known sin, but by the law: for I had not known lust, except the law had said, Thou shalt not covet." Romans 7:7.

To what law recorded in the Old Testament was Paul referring?

"Thou shalt not covet thy neighbour's house, thou shalt not covet thy neighbour's wife, nor his manservant, nor his maidservant, nor his ox, nor his ass, nor anything that *is* thy neighbour's." Exodus 20:17.

NOTE: *This is one of the Ten Commandments, given in Exodus 20:3-17.*

What does the Bible say sin is?

"Whosoever committeth sin transgresseth also the law: for sin is the transgression of the law." 1 John 3:4.

Can sin exist when there is no law?

"Because the law worketh wrath: for where no law is, *there is* no transgression." Romans 4:15.

NOTE: God gave His perfect law to point out sin. In the Ten Commandments we have the perfect rule of right living. To the sinner it brings a conviction of sin. To the Christian it serves as a standard of right living. It does not save from sin—it can only bring a conviction of sin so that the sinner might feel his need of Christ and come to Him for salvation.

Because the transgression of God's law has made us sinners, what was it necessary for Christ to do?

"But God commendeth his love toward us, in that, while we were yet sinners, Christ died for us." Romans 5:8.

By what then are we saved from our sins?

"For by grace are ye saved through faith; and that not of yourselves: *it is* the gift of God: not of works, lest any man should boast." Ephesians 2:8, 9.

NOTE: Grace is defined as "unmerited favor." It is something that we cannot earn, nor do we deserve it. It is the tree gift of God.

How do we receive this gift of grace?

"For the wages of sin *is* death; but the gift of God *is* eternal life through Jesus Christ our Lord." Romans 6:23.

NOTE: Jesus exchanged places with us. On the cross He received the punishment that we deserve. Thus the debt of our sins was paid. We receive the reward His perfect life of obedience deserves.

How does Paul indicate that one saved by grace will not continue to live in sin?

"What shall we say then? Shall we continue in sin, that grace may abound? God forbid. How shall we, that are dead to sin live any longer therein? . . . For sin shall not have dominion over you: for ye are not under the law, but under grace. What then? shall we sin, because we are not under the law, but under grace? God forbid." Romans 6:1, 2, 14, 15.

Does our acceptance of Christ through faith abolish the law?

"Do we then make void the law through faith? God forbid: yea, we establish the law." Romans 3:31.

What nature do we still possess if we are opposed to God's law?

"Because the carnal mind *is* enmity against God: for it is not subject to the law of God, neither indeed can be." Romans 8:7.

How will the born-again person show his love for God?

"Whosoever believeth that Jesus is the Christ is born of God: and every one that loveth him that begat loveth him also that is begotten of him. By this we know that we love the children of God, when we love God, and keep his commandments. For this is the love of God, that we keep his commandments: and his commandments are not grievous." 1 John 5:1-3.

What does the Bible say about the person who professes to know Christ and yet refuses to obey Him?

"My little children, these things write I unto you, that ye sin not. And if any man sin, we have an advocate with the Father, Jesus Christ the righteous: and he is the propitiation for our sins: and not for our's only, but also for *the sins of* the whole world. And hereby we do know that we know him, if we keep his commandments. He that saith, I know him, and keepeth not his commandments, is a liar, and the truth is not in him." 1 John 2:1-4.

What will be the attitude of the person who has been saved by God's matchless grace?

"I delight to do thy will, O my God: yea, thy law *is* within my heart." Psalm 40:8.

One night in an evangelistic meeting a young man, who had been the town drunkard, responded to the appeal made and came forward, giving his life to Christ. When asked how he would solve the problems that faced him, he replied that he did not know, but he was determined to give himself to God.

His question was not, "How much must I give up to become a Christian?" It was, "How much can I do for Christ who did so much for me?" You see, Christ had taken full possession of that man's heart because a full surrender had been made. He had responded to the challenge of the Master when He said, "If any man will come after Me, let him deny himself, and take up his cross daily, and follow Me." Luke 9:23.

If you have not as yet accepted Christ as your Saviour, we invite you to do it now. Compare your life with the law of God and you will discover that you are a sinner. Learn from the Bible that the wages of sin is death. Realize that your only hope for cleansing and salvation is found in Christ and His death for your sins. Then come and kneel by faith at the cross and let Him take away your sins. Arise from your knees and go forth to live for Him. This is the only way you can find peace and happiness for your soul.

Why Not Talk To God About The Sabbath?

Tell me, Lord, do you have a special day of rest for your followers or is every day alike?

"I was in the Spirit on the Lord's day." Revelation 1:10.

But which day is the Lord's day? Which day are you Lord of?

"The Son of man is Lord even of the *Sabbath day*." Matthew 12:8.

There are seven days in the week. Which day is the Sabbath day?

"The *seventh day* is the Sabbath of the Lord thy God." Fourth commandment (Exodus 20:8.)

Which day, according to our reckoning, is the seventh day, Saturday or Sunday?

"And when the *Sabbath was past*, Mary Magdalene and Mary, the mother of James, . . . very early in the morning the *first day of the week*, they came unto the sepulchre at the rising of the sun . . . and entering into the sepulchre, they saw a young man . . . And he saith unto them, be not affrighted; Ye seek Jesus of Nazareth, which was crucified; *He is risen*." Mark 16:1-6.

NOTE: Everybody knows that Sunday was the resurrection day. The Sabbath was past when it dawned. Thus it is evident that Sabbath is Saturday, the day before Sunday.

But, Lord, didn't you abolish the law which contains the Sabbath Commandment?

"Do not suppose that I have come to do away with the law or the prophets. I have not come to do away with them, but to enforce them." Matthew 5:17 (Goodspeed).

Well, at least, didn't you change one of the Commandments so that today your followers may keep another day?

"I tell you, as long as heaven and earth endure, not one dotting of an 'i' or crossing of a 't' will be dropped from the law until it is all observed." Matthew 5:18 (Goodspeed).

But, Lord, isn't Saturday a Jewish day? Isn't the seventh day the Sabbath of the Jews?

"The Sabbath was made *for man*." Mark 2:27. (The Sabbath was made and given to man 2500 years ago before the existence of a Jew. See Genesis 2:1-3.)

Someone told me that after your crucifixion, your followers no longer kept the seventh-day Sabbath according to the Commandments. Is this true?

"And that day was the Preparation day and the Sabbath drew on. And the women also which came with Him from Galilee, followed after, and beheld the sepulchre, and how his body was laid. And they returned and prepared spices and ointments; and *rested the Sabbath day according to the commandment*." Luke 23:54-56.

But didn't the apostle Paul always meet with the early Christians on Sunday in honor of the Resurrection?

"And Paul, as his manner was, went in unto them, and three *Sabbath days* reasoned with them out of the Scriptures." Acts 17:2.

Perhaps he met with the Jews on the Sabbath and the Gentiles on Sunday. What about that?

"And he reasoned in the synagogue *every Sabbath*, and persuaded the *Jews and the Greeks*." Acts 18:4.

What did Paul teach in regard to Sabbath keeping?

"There therefore remaineth a keeping of the Sabbath (margin) to the people of God. For he that is entered into his rest, he also hath ceased from his own works as God did from His." Hebrews 4:9, 10.

But which day did Paul mean when he spoke of resting as God did?

"For He spake in a certain place of the *seventh day* on this wise, And God did rest the seventh day from all His works." Hebrews 4:4. (In the New Testament there are no less than 59 references on the Sabbath. The book of Acts records 84 Sabbaths on which the apostle Paul and his associates held religious services. Yet there is not one word in the entire Bible authorizing Sunday keeping.)

Why do so many people keep Sunday instead of Saturday? If the Bible teaches Sabbath keeping, how and by whom was Sunday keeping started?

"And he (the 'little horn' power) shall speak great words against the Most High, . . . and think to change times and laws." Daniel 7:25.

The Roman Catholic Church is the Little Horn of Daniel 7. Does it think it has the power to change the law of God?

"Had she not such power she could not have done that in which all modern religionists agree with her; she could not have substituted the observance of Sunday, the first day of the week, for the observance of Saturday, the seventh day of the week, a change for which there is no Scriptural authority." Stephen Keenan, a RC priest, *Doctrinal Catechism,* p. 174.

When was this change made?

"We observe Sunday instead of Saturday because the Catholic Church in the Council of Laodicea (346 A.D.) transferred the solemnity from Saturday to Sunday." Peter Geirmann, *The Converts' Catechism,* p. 50. (This catechism received the pope's blessing on January 25, 1910.)

Do Protestant ministers agree with this?
CONGREGATIONALIST: "It is quite clear that however rigidly or devotedly we may spend Sunday, we are not keeping the Sabbath."—Dr. R. W. Dale, *The Ten Commandments*, p. 106.

METHODIST: "Sabbath in the Hebrew language signifies rest and is the seventh day of the week. . . . and it must be confessed that there is no law in the New Testament concerning the first day."—Buck's *Theological Dictionary.*

BAPTIST: "There was and is a commandment to keep holy the Sabbath day, but that Sabbath day was not Sunday. It will be said, however, and with some show of triumph, that the Sabbath was transferred from the seventh to the first day of the week. . . . Where can the record of such a transfer be found? Not in the New Testament—absolutely not. . . . Of course, I quite well know that Sunday did come into use in early Christian history. . . . But what a pity that it comes branded with the mark of paganism, and christened with the name of the sun god, when adopted and sanctioned by the Papal apostasy, and bequeathed as a sacred legacy to Protestantism." Dr. E. T. Hiscox, author of the *Baptist Manual.*

What difference does it make which day I keep? A day is a day, isn't it?
"Know ye not that to whom ye yield yourselves servants to obey, his servants ye are to whom ye obey; whether of sin unto death, or of *obedience* unto righteousness?" Romans 6:16.

Then what shall I do, obey the Sabbath of God's Commandment or keep the Sunday of man?
"We ought to obey God rather than men." Acts 5:29.

Well, Lord, what do you think of Sunday keeping?

"Thus have ye made the commandment of God of none effect by your tradition . . . But in vain they do worship Me, teaching for doctrines the commandments of men." Matthew 15:6, 9.

But surely the millions of people who keep Sunday can't be wrong, can they?

"Enter ye in at the strait gate: for wide is the gate and broad is the way that leadeth to destruction and many there be which go in thereat: because strait is the gate and narrow is the way that leadeth unto life, and few there be that find it." Matthew 7:13, 14. (Only a few obeyed God in the days of Noah, in the days of Lot, in the days of Christ. The majority were lost.)

But Dr. So-And-So is a very wise man: Why doesn't he and all the great preachers keep the Sabbath?

"For ye see your calling, brethren, how that not many wise men after the flesh, not many mighty, not many noble, are called, but God hath chosen the foolish things of the world to confound the wise; and God hath chosen the weak things of the world to confound the things which are mighty." 1 Corinthians 1:26, 27.

NOTE: The great religious teachers in Christ's day rejected the truth also. His followers were of the common people.

But I have accepted Jesus. He has accepted me and I have been keeping Sunday. Surely I would not be lost if I did not keep the Sabbath now, would I?

"The times of *this ignorance* God winked at; but now commandeth all men every where to *repent*." Acts 17:30.

I know you, Lord, you wouldn't condemn me for breaking the Sabbath, would you?

"He that saith, I know Him, and keepeth not His commandments, is a liar, and the truth is not in Him." 1 John 2:4.

But isn't it sufficient that I love the Lord and live by the law of love?

"If ye love Me, keep My commandments." John 14:15.

Does that mean all ten of them?

"For whosoever shall keep the whole law, and yet offend in one point, he is guilty of all." James 2:10.

Well, I think that if we try to follow Jesus, that is all that is necessary. Isn't that right?

"He that saith he abideth in Him, ought himself also to walk, even as He walked." 1 John 2:6.

What was your custom regarding the Sabbath?

"And He came to Nazareth, where He had been brought up; and, as His custom was, He went to the synagogue on the Sabbath day and stood up for to read." Luke 4:16.

But, Lord, that was over 1900 years ago. Wouldn't you keep some other day than Saturday if you should come to earth today?

"I am the Lord, I change not." Malachi 3:6. "Jesus Christ, the same yesterday, and today, and forever." Hebrews 13:8.

Does my salvation depend upon my obedience to your Commandments?

"And being perfect, He became the author of eternal salvation unto *all them that obey him.*" Hebrews 5:9.

Is it absolutely necessary to keep the Commandments to receive Eternal Life?

"If thou will enter into life, keep the commandments." Matthew 19:17.

But I still can't see why you insist on the seventh day, Lord. Isn't Sunday as good as Saturday?

"God blessed the seventh day and sanctified." Genesis 2:3.

"He hath blessed and I cannot reverse it." Numbers 23:20.

"For thou blessest, O Lord, and it shall be blessed forever." 1 Chronicles 17:27.

Well, it seems to me that if I keep one day in seven, regardless of which one, that ought to be good enough.

"There is a way that seemeth right unto a man; but the end thereof are the ways of death." Proverbs 16:25. "Spiritual things . . . are spiritually discerned." 1 Corinthians 2:13, 14.

But, Lord! Can't I do something else? Won't my prayers and my profession get me to heaven?

"Not every one that saith unto Me, Lord, Lord shall enter into the kingdom of heaven, but he that doeth the will of My Father which is in heaven." Matthew 7:21.

But I pray.

"He that turneth away his ear from hearing the law, even his prayer shall be abomination." Proverbs 28:9.

But, Lord, look at the people who work miracles. Some heal the sick, others talk in tongues; yet they do not keep the Sabbath. What about them?

"Many will say to Me in that day, Lord, Lord, have we not prophesied in Thy name? And in Thy name have cast out devils? And in Thy name done many wonderful works? And then will I profess unto them, I never knew you: Depart from Me." Matthew 7:22, 23.

Yes, I know the Sabbath is right; but my business would suffer if I closed on Sabbath. I might lose my job.

"For what shall it profit a man if he shall gain the whole world and lose his own soul?" Mark 8:36.

Well, for myself I wouldn't care; but what about my family? Wouldn't it be better for me to work on the Sabbath than to let my family starve?

"Your heavenly Father knoweth that ye have need of all these things; but seek ye first the kingdom of God and His righteousness; and all these things shall be added unto you." Matthew 6:32, 33. "I have not seen the righteous forsaken, nor his seed begging bread." Psalm 37:25.

My friends will laugh at me and ridicule me.

"Blessed are ye, when men shall revile you, . . . and shall say all manner of evil against you falsely for My sake; rejoice, and be exceeding glad, for great is your reward in heaven." Matthew 5:11, 12.

"If the world hate you, ye know that it hated Me before it hated you." John 15:18.

But suppose my own family does not agree with me. Should I cause a division in my home?

"He that loveth father or mother more than Me is not worthy of Me: And he that loveth son or daughter more than Me is not worthy of Me. And he that taketh not his cross, and followeth after Me is not worthy of Me." Matthew 10:37, 38.

"So likewise, whosoever he be of you that forsaketh not all that he hath, he cannot be My disciple." Luke 14:33.

I am afraid I won't be able to withstand all these trials. I am too weak.

"My grace is sufficient for thee: for My strength is made perfect in weakness. . . . When I am weak, then am I strong." 2 Corinthians 12:9, 10. "I can do all things through Christ which strengtheneth me." Philippians 4:13.

Then, Lord, what is the reward for being faithful to you and the Commandments?

"There is no man that hath left house, or parents, or brethren, or wife, or children, for the kingdom of God's sake, who shall not receive manifold more in this present time, and in the world to come, life everlasting." Luke 18:29, 30. "Blessed are they that do His commandments that they may have right to the tree of life, and may enter in through the gates into the city." Revelation 22:14.

Lord, I'm looking forward to a home in the earth made new, will we keep the Sabbath there, too?

"For as the new heavens and the new earth which I will make shall remain before Me, saith the Lord, so shall your seed and your name remain; and it shall come to pass that from one new moon to another and *from one Sabbath to another* shall all flesh come to worship before Me, saith the Lord." Isaiah 66:22, 23.

Then, Lord, Thy will be done on earth as it is in heaven. With your help, I will keep the Sabbath.

"Well done, good and faithful servant." Matthew 25:21.

WHICH MARK WILL YOU RECEIVE?

"The Catholic Church for over one thousand years before the existence of a Protestant, by virtue of her divine mission, changed the day from Saturday to Sunday."—*Catholic Mirror*, September, 1893.

"Of course the Catholic Church claims that the change was her act. And the act is a MARK of her ecclesiastical power and authority in religious matters."—C. F. Thomas, Chancellor of Cardinal Gibbons.

"The observance of Sunday by the Protestants is an *homage* they pay in spite of themselves *to the authority of the Catholic Church.*"—*Plain Talk for Protestants,* page 213.

"And hallow My Sabbaths; and they shall be a SIGN between Me and you, that ye may know that I am the Lord your God." Ezekiel 20:20.

Prayers That Are Answered

During the second World War, a flyer shot down in the Pacific Ocean, floated for some time on a rubber raft without being found. Finally, in desperation he prayed this prayer, "Dear God, I haven't asked you for anything for twenty years. If you will hear my prayer and send someone to rescue me; I won't trouble you for another twenty years."

One writer has said that too many people treat God like a lawyer or a physician. They go to Him only when they are in trouble or sick. Many people think of prayer as being something to save until a person is in great trouble and cannot find help any place else.

Prayer is the means by which those who live on earth can communicate with their Father who is in heaven. Christ, while here on earth, missed the daily communion with God that he had enjoyed in heaven. He spent whole nights in prayer, for this was His way of talking with His Father.

Adam, before he fell, was able each evening to walk and talk with God. Sin separated man from his heavenly Father as far as face-to-face communion was concerned, but God then gave man the privilege to talk with Him in prayer. What a privilege it is to commune with our heavenly Father at any time and under any circumstance.

God longs for us to open our hearts to Him and bring our problems to Him for His help. Let us discover how we can talk with God so that our prayers will be heard and answered.

What did the disciples ask Jesus to do for them?

"And it came to pass, that, as he was praying in a certain place, when he ceased, one of his disciples said unto him, Lord, teach us to pray, as John also taught his disciples." Luke 11:1.

NOTE: Like the disciples, we need to learn from God to pray as Christ prayed, that God might hear and answer our petitions.

To whom should we pray?

"And he said unto them, When ye pray, say, Our Father which art in heaven, Hallowed be thy name. Thy kingdom come. Thy will be done, as in heaven, so in earth." Luke 11:2.

In whose name can we confidently approach the throne of God in prayer?

"If ye shall ask any thing in my name, I will do it." John 14:14.

NOTE: It is through the merit of Christ's perfect life that we can confidently approach God in prayer.

With what should our prayers be mingled?

"Be careful for nothing; but in every thing by prayer and supplication with thanksgiving let your requests be made known unto God." Philippians 4:6.

How sincerely must we seek God in our prayers?

"Then shall ye call upon me, and ye shall go and pray unto me, and I will hearken unto you. And ye shall seek me, and find *me*, when ye shall search for me with all your heart." Jeremiah 29:12, 13.

What assurance do we have that God will hear and answer our prayers?

"Ask, and it shall be given you; seek, and ye shall find; knock, and it shall be opened unto you: For every one that asketh receiveth; and he that seeketh findeth; and to him that knocketh it shall be opened." Matthew 7:7, 8.

How willing is God to answer the prayers of His people?

"If ye then, being evil, know how to give good gifts unto your children, how much more shall your Father which is in heaven give good things to them that ask him?" Matthew 7:11.

What help is promised to the child of God that his prayers might be understood and answered by God?

"Likewise the Spirit also helpeth our infirmities: for we know not what we should pray for as we ought: but the Spirit itself maketh intercession for us with groanings which cannot be uttered." Romans 8:26.

What condition did Christ say is necessary before our prayers will be heard?

"Therefore I say unto you, What things soever ye desire, when ye pray, believe that ye receive *them*, and ye shall have *them*." Mark 11:24.

If we lack faith when we pray, what does the Bible say will be the result?

"But let them ask in faith, nothing wavering. For he that wavereth is like a wave of the sea driven with the wind and tossed. For let not that man think that he shall receive any thing of the Lord." James 1:6, 7.

What petitions may we expect God to answer?

"And this is the confidence that we have in him, that, if we ask any thing according to his will, he heareth us: And if we know that he hear us, whatsoever we ask, we know that we have the petitions that we desired of him." 1 John 5:14, 15.

Why are some of our prayers not answered as we would like?

"Ye ask, and receive not, because ye ask amiss, that ye may consume *it* upon your lusts." James 4:3.

Under what conditions does the Lord refuse to hear our prayers?

"If I regard iniquity in my heart, the Lord will not hear me." Psalm 66:18.

Whose prayers will be an abomination to the Lord?

"He that turneth away his ear from hearing the law, even his prayer *shall be* abomination." Proverbs 28:9.

How often should Christians pray?

"Praying always with all prayer and supplication in the Spirit, and watching thereunto me with all perseverance and supplication for all saints." Ephesians 6:18.

"Pray without ceasing." 1 Thessalonians 5:17.

When did David set aside special times for prayer?

"Evening, and morning, and at noon, will I pray, and cry aloud: and he shall hear my voice." Psalm 55:17.

One writer has said that prayer is the opening of the heart to God as to a friend. It is sharing life's joys and woes with One who loves and cares. What a privilege to share our innermost thoughts with God!

On holidays it is often difficult to telephone a loved one because most circuits are already busy with calls placed by loved ones across the country. What a privilege it is to talk to one that is near and dear to you even though separated by many miles. Millions of dollars are spent each year by the American people because they want to talk to those they love.

It costs nothing but a little time spent on our knees to talk to the King of the Universe. How often we carry needless burdens and problems because we have not taken the time to pray! Let us decide today that our prayer life is going to be a rich, rewarding experience as we use it to become acquainted with our God. The circuits to the King of the Universe are never busy; there is always an opening for our sincere prayer.

God's Money In My Wallet

When Christ began His ministry in Jerusalem, one of the first things he did was to drive the money changers out of the temple. We find that three and a half years later, as he neared the end of His ministry, the money changers had returned to the temple. Notice what the Bible says Christ did, "And Jesus went into the temple of God and cast out all of them that sold and bought in the temple, and overthrew the table of the money changers, and the seats of them that sold doves. And said unto them. It is written, My house shall be called a house of prayer, but ye have made it a den of thieves." Matthew 21:12, 13.

If the Lord were to visit many churches today He would say the same thing that He did 1900 years ago. Not long ago a newspaper told about a pastor of a large church who found himself short of funds to operate his church. He devised a most ingenious scheme to raise the needed funds. He had printed raffle tickets and sold chances on a case of 90 proof whiskey. Some good member of his church, after having been taught how to gamble by his minister, would be the proud possessor of a case of whiskey by which he could become intoxicated.

Some religionists defend such practices by saying they are necessary in order to finance the giving of the gospel. It would not be necessary to stoop to such depths of iniquity if we would take the Bible and let God show His plan for giving of the gospel.

What is God's plan for providing for His work?

"Bring ye all the tithes into the storehouse, that there may be meat in mine house, and prove me now herewith, saith the Lord of hosts, if I will not open you the windows of heaven, and pour you out a blessing, that *there shall* not *be room* enough *to receive it.*" Malachi 3:10.

How did Abraham show that he recognized the tithing system?

"And Melchizedek king of Salem brought forth bread and wine: and he *was* the priest of the most high God. And he blessed him, and said, Blessed *be* Abram of the most high God, possessor of heaven and earth: And blessed be the most high God, which hath delivered thine enemies into thy hand. And he gave him tithes of all." Genesis 14:18-20.

NOTE: Hebrews 7:1, 2 also tells us that Abraham gave a tenth of all. The tithe is the tenth.

What portion of his income did Jacob promise God for blessings received?

"And Jacob vowed a vow, saying, If God will be with me, and will keep me in this way that I go, and will give me bread to eat, and raiment to put on, so that I come again to my father's house in peace, then shall the Lord be my God: And this stone, which I have set *for* a pillar, shall be God's house: and of all that thou shalt give me I will surely give the tenth unto thee." Genesis 28:20-22.

For what purpose was the tithe to be used during the days of ancient Israel?

"And, behold, I have given the children of Levi all the tenth in Israel for an inheritance, for their service which they serve, *even* the service of the tabernacle of the congregation. . . . But the tithes of the children of Israel, which they offer as an heave offering unto the Lord, I have given to the Levites to inherit: therefore I have said unto them, Among the children of Israel they shall have no inheritance." Numbers 18:21, 24.

To whom does the tithe belong?

"And all the tithe of the land, *whether* of the seed of the land, *or* of the fruit of the tree, *is* the Lord's: *it is* holy unto the Lord. . . . And concerning the tithe of the herd, or of the flock, *even* of whatsoever passeth under the rod, the tenth shall be holy unto the Lord." Leviticus 27:30, 32.

Upon what basis does God claim the tithe as rightfully His?

"The earth is the Lord's, and the fulness thereof; the world, and they that dwell therein." Psalm 24:1.

"For every beast of the forest *is* mine, *and* the cattle upon a thousand hills. I know all the fowls of the mountains: and the wild beasts of the field *are* mine. If I were hungry, I would not tell thee: for the world *is* mine, and the fulness thereof." Psalm 50:10-12.

Who gives us the ability to earn a living?

"But thou shalt remember the Lord thy God: for *it is* he that giveth thee power to get wealth, that he may establish his covenant which he sware unto thy fathers, as *it is* this day." Deuteronomy 8:18.

What should be our response to the Lord for all that He has entrusted to us?

"Honour the Lord with thy substance, and with the firstfruits of all thine increase: so shall thy barns be filled with plenty, and thy presses shall burst out with new wine." Proverbs 3:9, 10.

What did Jesus say concerning the faithfulness of the Jews in paying tithe?

"Woe unto you, scribes and Pharisees, hypocrites! for ye pay tithe of mint and anise and cummin, and have omitted the weightier *matters* of the law, judgment, mercy, and faith: these ought ye to have done, and not to leave the other undone." Matthew 23:23.

NOTE: While pointing out their failures, Jesus endorses tithe paying.

How does Paul say the Christian minister is to be supported?

"Do ye not know that they which minister about holy things live *of the things* of the temple? and they which wait at the altar are partakers with the altar? Even so hath the Lord ordained that they which preach the gospel should live of the gospel." 1 Corinthians 9:13, 14.

What does a man do when he withholds tithe and offerings from God?

"Will a man rob God? Yet ye have robbed me. But ye say, Wherein have we robbed thee? In tithes and offerings. Ye *are* cursed with a curse: for ye have robbed me, *even* this whole nation." Malachi 3:8, 9.

What blessings does He promise to those who will be faithful in recognizing His ownership?

"Bring ye all the tithes into the storehouse, that there may be meat in mine house, and prove me now herewith, saith the Lord of hosts, if I will not open you the windows of heaven, and pour you out a blessing, that *there shall* not *be room* enough to *receive it.* And I will rebuke the devourer for your sakes, and he shall not destroy the fruits of your ground; neither shall your vine cast her fruit before the time in the field, saith the Lord of hosts." Malachi 3:10, 11.

When are we to think of God and our obligation to Him?

"But seek ye first the kingdom of God, and his righteousness; and all these things shall be added unto you." Matthew 6:33.

How will God reward the liberal giver?

"Give, and it shall be given unto you; good measure, pressed down, and shaken together, and running over, shall men give into your bosom. For with the same measure that ye mete withal it shall be measured to you again." Luke 6:38.

Where does God advise us to deposit our treasures?

"Lay not up for yourselves treasures upon earth, where moth and rust doth corrupt, and where thieves break through and steal: But lay up for yourselves treasures in heaven, where neither moth nor rust doth corrupt, and where thieves do not break through nor steal: For where your treasure is there will your heart be also." Matthew 6:19-21.

Thousands of stories could be told about those who have tried God's plan and who have discovered that God's promises are sure. A farmer had always been faithful in returning to God a tithe. One day he saw a dark cloud of locusts in the sky and knew that it was headed toward his farm. If the locusts ate his crop he faced financial ruin. With his family gathered about him that evening he reminded God of the promise in Malachi 3:10, 11. The family went to bed that night and slept secure in the knowledge that their heavenly Father never sleeps, but watches over His own.

The next morning the farmer arose to examine his fields. He discovered that the locusts had eaten to his fence on every side, but not a green stem was left on the other side of the fence. God had kept His promise and protected the faithful farmer's crop from the locusts.

What better insurance can a man have against disaster, costly sicknesses, or accident than a partnership with the all-powerful God? Try God's plan and you will never again be without the blessings that come as you and God become partners.

As you meditate upon this subject, pause first to count your many blessings. Remember that every good and perfect gift comes from God.

The Truth About Hell

Many years ago a bridegroom and his bride were enjoying the happy occasion of their wedding feast. According to the custom the bridegroom's friend served the newly wedded couple with drinks. But the cup that the friend gave the bridegroom was mingled with poison. Now there was death in the air. The laughing and rejoicing of this festive wedding reception would soon be turned into weeping and mourning. The murderer quickly stole away, took the fastest horse and fled for his life into the forest. All night he whipped and goaded his speeding horse to escape arrest and punishment by the pursuing police. Farther and farther he got away, so he thought. But just as dawn was breaking, he came out of the forest with his horse foaming with sweat. He looked up and was horrified. The castle, the place of the wedding feast, was right in front of him. He had ridden hard and fast, but he had ridden round and round. He thought he was fleeing from his crime, but he was only returning to it.

We cannot get away from our sin unless God takes it from us. We cannot walk, run, or fly fast enough to escape it. Unless it is forgiven and covered with the atoning blood of Christ, it will go to the grave with us and arise to face us in the judgment. We can never outrace it, but we can give it up and in God's mercy find redemption.

The time is coming, Jesus says, when there will be a great separation in the human race. Both the righteous and wicked will be treated justly and fairly in this separation and judgment. The reward of the righteous is everlasting life. The punishment of the wicked is eternal destruction.

Through misrepresentation of the character of God millions of people believe that God is cruel and eagerly waiting to punish men. The Bible, contrary to human opinion, sweeps away these false conceptions and makes clear that God is a God of mercy and love, even in His punishment of the sinner. Let us discover what the Bible really teaches concerning hell, the punishment of the wicked.

What does the Bible teach about the time of punishment for the wicked?

"The Lord knoweth how to deliver the godly out of temptations, and to reserve the unjust unto the day of judgment to be punished." 2 Peter 2:9.

NOTE: *The Dictionary defines "reserve": "To retain or hold over to a future time." "To be punished" also refers to something that will take place in the future.*

When does Jesus say this "day of judgment" will take place?

"The enemy that sowed them is the devil; the harvest is the end of the world; and the reapers are the angels. As therefore the tares are gathered and burned in the fire; so shall it be in the end of this world. The Son of man shall send forth his angels, and they shall gather out of his kingdom all things that offend, and them which do iniquity; and shall cast them into a furnace of fire: there shall be wailing and gnashing of teeth." Matthew 13:39-42.

"When the Son of man shall come in his glory, and all the holy angels with him, then shall he sit upon the throne of his glory." Matthew 25:31.

In what place will the fires of hell punish the wicked?

"But the heavens and the earth, which are now, by the same word are kept in store, reserved unto fire against the day of judgment and perdition of ungodly men." 2 Peter 3:7.

NOTE: Justice demands that a man be punished in the place where the crime was committed, and the Bible makes plain that the wicked will burn right here on earth. Revelation 20:9; 2 Peter 3:10.

After the fires of hell have burned out what glorious scene will appear?

"Nevertheless we, according to his promise, look for new heavens and a new earth, wherein dwelleth righteousness." 2 Peter 3:13.

In what words does the Bible indicate the length of time God will cause the burning fire of hell to punish the unsaved or wicked?

"For, behold, the day cometh, that shall burn as an oven; and all the proud, yea, and all that do wickedly, shall be stubble: and the day that cometh shall burn them up, saith the Lord of hosts, that it shall leave them neither root nor branch. . . . And ye shall tread down the wicked; for they shall be ashes under the soles of your feet in the day that I shall do *this*, saith the Lord of hosts." Malachi 4:1, 3.

After the wicked are destroyed, how much of the fire will be left?

"Behold, they shall be as stubble; the fire shall burn them; they shall not deliver themselves from the power of the flame: *there shall* not *be* a coal to warm at, *nor* fire to sit before it." Isaiah 47:14.

NOTE: A fire goes out when there is no more fuel to burn. The fire that burns the wicked goes out when they are completely reduced to ashes.

Jesus speaks of the wicked going "into everlasting fire" or "punishment." Matthew 25:41, 46. How does God's destruction of the ancient cities of Sodom and Gomorrha make clear the meaning of these terms?

"Even as Sodom and Gomorrha, and the cities about them in like manner, giving themselves over to fornication, and going after strange flesh, are set forth for an example, suffering the vengeance of eternal fire." Jude 7.

"And turning the cities of Sodom and Gomorrha into ashes condemned *them* with an overthrow, making *them* an ensample unto those that after should live ungodly." 2 Peter 2:6.

NOTE: The first text says these cities were burned with "eternal fire." The second tells that they were reduced to "ashes." So the Bible explains that the results of this fire is everlasting. Even if the meaning of some Bible texts may not seem entirely clear, other Bible references explain their meaning.

The prophet Jonah tells of his experience in the belly of a great fish. (a) What word did Jonah use to describe his length of time beneath the waters, and (b) how long does the Bible say this period actually lasted?

(a) "I went down to the bottoms of the mountains; the earth with her bars was about me for ever; yet hast thou brought up my life from corruption, O Lord my God." Jonah 2:6. (b) "Now the Lord had prepared a great fish to swallow up Jonah. And Jonah was in the belly of the fish three days and three nights." Jonah 1:17.

NOTE: Exodus 21:6 tells about a Hebrew slave who at the end of seven years had the privilege of gaining his freedom. However, if the slave loved his master and did not want to go free, he could choose to "serve him forever." "Forever" meant that the servant would serve his master as long as he lived, a lifetime. Thus, the Bible is its own interpreter, and makes plain that God will not torture the wicked with unending punishment.

(a) Does God want anyone to be lost and (b) what is His desire for all men?

(a) "The Lord is not slack concerning his promise, as some men count slackness; but is longsuffering to usward, not willing that any should perish, (b) but that all should come to repentance." 2 Peter 3:9

What are the two great rewards for the human race?

"For the wages of sin *is* death, but the gift of God *is* eternal life through Jesus Christ our Lord." Romans 6:23.

God so loved the world that He sent His Son to die for us. Jesus has paid the price for our redemption, but God will not force us to accept Christ as our Saviour. If we want forgiveness and cleansing, we can have it. On the other hand, if we are determined to continue in sin, God cannot save us. "How shall we escape if we neglect so great salvation?" Hebrews 2:3.

God is not only merciful, but He is a God of justice. If a person refuses the free gift of salvation, he will be destroyed. The person who clings to his sins would not be happy in heaven. Only those who have learned to love righteousness will desire to be there.

Every year thousands of young people study hard for their baccalaureate exams, hoping they can pass. They know that a diploma opens the door for higher education, a good job, and a big salary. But only a minority pass. Most find the doors closed to them.

The door to heaven is wide open. God doesn't want to fail anyone. His examination is very easy. Here it is: "If ye be WILLING AND OBEDIENT ye shall eat the good of the land." Anyone who really wants to pass this examination will succeed.

The decision is up to us individually whether we spend eternity in heaven or are destroyed. We can choose to love and obey God, or we can choose to neglect or refuse His great salvation. If we will seek His help, Jesus will create in us a desire to do His will. Won't you accept Jesus today and prepare to become a citizen of God's wonderful new world?

Hope Beyond the Grave

By Manny Piedad Mullaneda

My father suffered cancer of the liver, and the attending physician had pronounced his case as terminal - his days numbered. As he struggled for life, the excruciating pain made his breathing the last two nights so difficult, exhaustive, and agonizing that brought the members of our family close to his bed side.

"Where are you going?" he asked with feeble and dainty voice as I readied to go out next morning. "I'll go out for a while; will be back the soonest." I replied.

On my way back home, someone broke the news of his death. I rushed home and tried to wake him up hoping what someone said was not final. I called him through his ears, and shook his shoulders for possible response, but to no avail. If not in his lifeless body, was he listening somewhere?

My father passed away in his hometown Madrid, Surigao del Sur, Philippines a day before his 69th birthday. He was a man of humanitarian concern, and to prove this altruistic service, he was the one who worked for the conversion of Bayugan, Agusan del Sur into a municipality in 1960. He, the first appointed town mayor, and being the founder has been remembered during foundation days of the said town. Aside from this, he also had endeavored to elevate two other places to the status of town, the last one of which he was processing almost to hit the finishing line at the time he was dying. Thus I could see a large number of sympathizers thronging to take the last glimpse of him, and a long line following the casket to his temporary resting place.

I recalled when I went home from work for a week-end, he would wake me up as early as about 2:00 o'clock in the morning to show me some documents he treasured much, and wanted to share with me being the only son of four. I rose up with eyelids still heavy. I forced to open my eyes wider, but the thing didn't arrest my interest. He talked and talked while my mind was set on the pillow. Then my mother reprimanded my father for robbing me to sleep. Disappointed, he silently folded the papers and carefully placed back to the folder. As he laid back, I could sense his eyes looking further beyond while on deep thought.

Now that he has expired, I tried to look over the papers and began to appreciate his efforts, though some lines supposedly need his personal explanation. I want him now to talk again and give him my rapt attention. I missed him very much! Too bad that when he asked where I was going that morning, it turned out to be my last to hear his fainting baritone voice.

Are the dead alive? Can we see and talk with them again? Do they go direct either to heaven or hell immediately after death?

King David died but did not go to heaven. "Men and brethren let me freely speak unto you of the patriarch David that he is both dead and buried, and his sepulcher (body) is with us unto this day. For David is not ascended into the heavens..." *(Acts 2:29, 34).*

Lazarus died, but resurrected four days later... Jesus saith unto them, our friend Lazarus sleepeth, but I go, that I may awake him out of sleep. Then said Jesus unto them plainly, Lazarus was dead. Take ye away the stone. Martha, the sister of him that was dead, saith unto Him, Lord by this time he stinketh: for he hath been dead four days... And when He thus spoken, he cried with a loud voice, Lazarus, come forth. And that was dead came forth bound hand and foot with grave clothes: and his face was bound about with a napkin. Jesus saith unto them. Loose him, and let him go: (John 11:11, 14, 39, 43, and 44). Lazarus said nothing of having gone to heaven.

Jesus died and was buried. In the third day he arose from the dead. After a week-end in the tomb, Jesus told Mary that He had not yet ascended to His father. *"Touch me not; for I am not yet ascended to my father; but go to my brethren, and say unto them, I ascend unto my father, and your Father, and to my God, and your God." (John 20:17).* While buried, Jesus was not in heaven.

THE DEAD KNOW NOT ANYTHING

"For the living know that they shall die: but the DEAD KNOW NOT ANYTHING, neither have they any more reward; for the memory of them is forgotten. Also their love, and their hatred, and their envy, is now perished; neither have they any more a portion forever in anything that is done under the sun." (Ecclesiastes 9:5-6). How can we talk with those who know not anything? They can't love, hate, and envy. The dead can't think and talk.

Those who claim to have communicated with departed loved ones, the voice from the other end must be that of an evil angel. One-third of the angelic population in heaven has been cast down to this earth with Lucifer *("His tail drew the third part of the stars in heaven." Revelation 12:4)*, and are actively deceiving people. These fallen intelligences can imitate the voice and actions of some deceased individuals whose peculiarities they observed while still alive. We know of some gifted persons who have the ability to reproduce the voice of other people; how much more for the fallen angels who were created a little higher than man! "For Thou has made man little lower than angels." (Psalms 8:5).

As E.G. White, a writer and religious leader puts it: "The fallen angels who do Satan's bidding appear as messengers from the spirit world. While professing to bring the living into communication with the dead, the prince of evil exercises his bewitching influence upon their minds. Satan has power to bring before men the appearance of their departed friends. The counterfeit is perfect; the familiar look, the words, the tone, are reproduced with marvelous distinction. Many are comforted with the assurance that their loved ones are enjoying the bliss of heaven; and without suspicion of danger, they give ear to "seducing spirits, and doctrines of devils". - The Final War p. 96

EVIL ANGELS AS MEDIUM TO TAKE THE PLACE OF BIBLES

We must understand the state of the dead for the spirits of devils (evil angels) will yet appear professing to be beloved friends and relatives who will declare words contrary to what the Bible says. When tempted by *Satan, Jesus successfully refuted; He repeatedly used the phrase* "It is written". (Matthew 4:4, 6). *The Bible is the final authority.*

In the garden of Eden, "The *Lord God commanded the man, "You are free to eat from any tree in the garden; but you must not eat from the tree of the knowledge of good and evil, for when you eat of it you will surely die." (Genesis 2:16, 17).* On the contrary, the devil said to the woman: *"You shall not surely die" (Genesis 3:4).* The devil's message was plain and simple: that soul is immortal. To believe that upon man's death, his soul continuous to live and goes somewhere, is to accept the doctrine on the immortality of the soul.

If some people would say: "Look, the dead has come back!" we must be prepared to withstand this wrong belief with the Bible truth that "the dead know not anything", and that they who thus appear are the spirits of devils. Satan is working with all power and signs and lying wonders, and with all deceivableness of unrighteousness" (2 Thessalonians 2:9, 10).

SHALL WE SEE OUR DEPARTED LOVED ONES AGAIN?

Yes! Those who shall be in heaven shall recognize father, mother, brother, sister, relatives and friends. Jesus shall be there! "for the Lord Himself shall descend from heaven with a shout with the voice of the archangel, and with the trump of God; and the dead in Christ shall rise first: Then we which are alive and remain shall be caught up together with them in the clouds to meet the Lord in the air: and so shall we ever be with the Lord: (1 Thessalonians 4:16, 17). In heaven, "God shall wipe away all tears from their eyes; and there shall be no more death, neither sorrow, nor crying, neither shall there be any more pain: for the former things are passed away" (Revelation 21:4).

Inscribed in front of my father's tomb is: "In loving memory of Sergio D. Mullaneda born October 7, 1913 died October 6, 1982". He is buried "sleeping in the ground just like Lazarus, patriarch David and others who are waiting for the resurrection morning when Christ shall come again. Of course, *the dead in Christ shall rise first" (1 Thessalonians 4:16).*

1,000 Years Of Peace

"The devil is bound, and we are now in the millennium," someone claimed.

"If the devil is bound," another replied, "he must be tied with a rubber chain that stretches from Paris to Bombay and from Washington, D.C., to the Kremlin."

We need only to look at what is happening about us to know that the devil has never been more active than he is today. Never have crime and sin been more widespread.

However, there is coming a time when the devil's activities will be justly restricted. He will be unable to tempt, torment, or destroy any of God's children. This is the day for which the whole world has longed. There will be perfect peace and happiness in the universe. The devil will be bound.

This period of one thousand years is called the millennium. This term is not found in the Bible. It comes from two Latin words, "mille" and "annus," and means 1,000 years. The phrase "1,000 years" is found six times in Revelation, chapter 20.

Many ideas about what is to occur during the millennium have been advanced. Some think of it as a thousand years of peace. However, we do not need to wonder; the Bible explains the period—its beginning, its purpose, and its end.

Before you begin the study of the questions in this lesson, read the entire twentieth chapter of Revelation.

In what two resurrections did Christ say the dead will be raised?

"Marvel not at this: for the hour is coming, in the which all that are in the graves shall hear his voice, and shall come forth; they that have done good, unto the resurrection of life; and they that have done evil, unto the resurrection of damnation." John 5:28, 29.

When will the righteous dead be raised?

"For the Lord himself shall descend from heaven with a shout, with the voice of the archangel, and with the trump of God: and the dead in Christ shall rise first: Then we which are alive *and* remain shall be caught up together with them in the clouds, to meet the Lord in the air: and so shall we ever be with the Lord." 1 Thessalonians 4:16, 17.

What does the Bible call this resurrection?

"Blessed and holy *is* he that hath part in the first resurrection: on such the second death hath no power, but they shall be priests of God and of Christ, and shall reign with him a thousand years." Revelation 20:6.

What happens to the living righteous when Christ's coming begins the millennium?

"Then we which are alive *and* remain shall be caught up together with them in the clouds, to meet the Lord in the air: and so shall we ever be with the Lord." 1 Thessalonians 4:17.

How does the Bible indicate that the righteous dead are raised at the beginning of the millennium?

"And I saw thrones, and they sat upon them, and judgment was given unto them: and *I saw* the souls of them that were beheaded for the witness of Jesus, and for the Word of God, and which had not worshipped the beast, neither his image, neither had received his mark upon their foreheads, or in their hands; and they lived and reigned with Christ a thousand years. . . . Blessed and holy is he that hath part in the first resurrection: on such the second death hath no power, but they shall be priests of God and of Christ, and shall reign with him a thousand years." Revelation 20:4, 6.

What effect does the coming of Christ have on the living wicked?

"And to you who are troubled rest with us, when the Lord Jesus shall be revealed from heaven with his mighty angels, in flaming fire taking vengeance on them that know not God, and that obey not the gospel of our Lord Jesus Christ: who shall be punished with everlasting destruction from the presence of the Lord, and from the glory of his power." 2 Thessalonians 1:7-9.

__NOTE:__ These are slain by the brightness of His coming. Sinful man is unable to stand before a sinless God. 2 Thessalonians 2:7, 8.

How does the Bible indicate that the second coming of Christ does not disturb the wicked dead?

"But the rest of the dead lived not again until the thousand years were finished. This *is* the first resurrection." Revelation 20:5.

Because Satan is bound, what is he unable to do during the millennium?

"And cast him into the bottomless pit, and shut him up, and set a seal upon him, that he should deceive the nations no more, till the thousand years should be fulfilled: and after that he must be loosed a little season." Revelation 20:3.

__NOTE:__ Satan is bound by "chains of darkness." He has no one to tempt or to destroy. The saints are with Christ in the New Jerusalem; the wicked living have died at the coming of Christ, and the wicked dead are not raised until the end of the millennium Satan and his wicked angels are alone on the earth during the 1,000 years. They have no human beings to tempt or deceive.

Where are the saints during the millennium?

"And I saw thrones, and they sat upon them, and judgment was given unto them: and *I* saw the souls of them that were beheaded for the witness of Jesus, and for the word of God, and which had not worshipped the beast, neither his image, neither had received *his* mark upon their foreheads, or in their hands; and they lived and reigned with Christ a thousand years. . . . Blessed and holy is he that hath part in the first resurrection: on such the second death hath no power, but they shall be priests of God and of Christ, and shall reign with him a thousand years." Revelation 20:4, 6.

How many people will there be upon the earth during the millennium?

"I beheld the earth, and, lo, *it was* without form and void; and the heavens, and they had no light. I beheld the mountains, and, lo, they trembled, and all the hills moved lightly. I beheld, and, lo, *there was* no man, and all the birds of the heavens were fled. I beheld, and lo, the fruitful place was a wilderness, and all the cities thereof were broken down at the presence of the Lord *and by* his fierce anger. For thus hath the Lord said, The whole land shall be desolate; yet will I not make a full end." Jeremiah 4:23-27.

When Christ returns with the saints at the end of the millennium, what happens to the Mount of Olives?

"And his feet shall stand in that day upon the mount of Olives, which is before Jerusalem on the east, and the mount of Olives shall cleave in the midst thereof toward the east and toward the west, *and there shall be* a great valley; and half of the mountain shall remove toward the north, and half of it toward the south. And ye shall flee *to* the valley of the mountains for the valley of the mountains shall reach unto Azal: yea, ye shall flee, like as ye fled from before the earthquake in the days of Uzziah king of Judah: and the Lord my God shall come, *and* all the saints with thee." Zechariah 14:4, 5.

What descends to fill the great plain made as Christ's feet touch the Mount of Olives?

"And I John saw the holy city, new Jerusalem, coming down from God out of heaven, prepared as a bride adorned for her husband." Revelation 21:2.

When does the Bible say that the wicked dead will live again?

"But the rest of the dead lived not again until the thousand years were finished. This *is* the first resurrection." Revelation 20:5.

When the resurrection of the wicked permits Satan to become active once more, what does he do to show that he has not changed?

"And when the thousand years are expired, Satan shall be loosed out of his prison, and shall go out to deceive the nations which are in the four quarters of the earth, Gog and Magog, to gather them together to battle: the number of whom *is* as the sand of the sea." Revelation 20:7, 8.

What is the outcome of Satan's attempt to take the city of God?

"And they went up in the breadth of the earth, and compassed the camp of the saints about, and the beloved city: and fire came down from God out of heaven, and devoured them . . . And death and hell were cast into the lake of fire. This is the second death. And whosoever was not found written in the book of life was cast into the lake of fire." Revelation 20:9, 14, 15.

After the purifying fire is over and all sin has been eliminated, what will God give man?

"But the day of the Lord will come as a thief in the night; in the which the heavens shall pass away with a great noise, and the elements shall melt with fervent heat, the earth also and the works that are therein shall be burned up. *Seeing* then *that* all these things shall be dissolved, what manner of *persons* ought ye to be in *all* holy conversation and godliness, looking for and hasting unto the coming of the day of

God, wherein the heavens being on fire shall be dissolved, and the elements shall melt with fervent heat? Nevertheless we, according to his promise, look for new heavens and a new earth, wherein dwelleth righteousness." 2 Peter 3:10-13.

I. Events at the beginning of the millennium:
   (a) Christ comes, righteous dead resurrected. 1 Thessalonians 4:16.
   (b) Righteous living changed. 1 Corinthians 15:51, 52.
   (c) Righteous living caught up with resurrected righteous to meet the Lord in the air. 1 Thessalonians 4:17.
   (d) Living wicked slain 2 Thessalonians 2:7, 8.
   (e) Satan bound for 1,000 years. Revelation 20:2.

II. Events during the millennium:
   (a) Saints reign with Christ and judge the wicked dead. Revelation 20:4; 1 Corinthians 6:2, 3.
   (b) Earth desolate Jeremiah 4:23-27.

III. Events at the close of the millennium:
   (a) Christ descends upon the Mount of Olives. Zechariah 14:4, 5.
   (b) New Jerusalem and saints descend. Revelation 21:2.
   (c) Satan loosed as wicked are raised. Revelation 20:7, 8.
   (d) Wicked destroyed by fire. Revelation 20:9, 15.
   (e) "New heaven and a new earth." Revelation 21:1.

Friend, where will you be at the end of the millennium? With Christ and the saved in the city, or with the wicked outside? By accepting Him now, you can make reservations for the future. Won't you decide today? Tomorrow may be too late. What is your response?

How To Postpone
Your Funeral

We have the following pertinent thoughts on the relationship of religion and health: "Most people have befuddled ideas on the relationship of religion and health. Either they snub their health completely, thinking that religion is of the spirit and has nothing to do with how you function physically; or they treat God as their personal magician who is to see to it that religion keeps them happy and well—free from moods of depression or discomfort, even though these be the result of their own wrong habits, . . . God's purpose is to make man whole. This process cannot be a one-dimensional project. You cannot have a full religious experience while your physical body is abused, debauched, and maltreated, just as you cannot have a full religious experience while your mind and spirit are defiled, ravished, and prostituted. A thorough-going religious experience should tone up the body, illuminate the mind, and free the spirit—until all three move in one rhythmical, harmonious entity—free from disease, and sanctified."—W. R. Beach in *Dimensions in Salvation*, pp. 264, 265.

Are health principles really a part of true Bible religion?

"Beloved, I wish above all things that thou mayest prosper and be in health, even as thy soul prospereth." 3 John 2.

There is a direct connection between sound health and bodily health. "Without health, no one can as distinctly understand or as completely fulfill his obligations to himself, to his fellow beings, or to his Creator. Therefore, the health should be faithfully guarded as the character."—*Education*, p. 195.

In fact, the Bible rates health right at the top of the list in importance. Man's mind, spiritual nature and body are all interrelated and interdependent. What affects one, affects the others. If man's body is misused, his mind and spiritual nature cannot become what God ordained that they should be.

Why did God give health rules to His people?

"And the Lord commanded us to do all these statutes . . . for our good always, that he might preserve us alive." Deuteronomy 6:24. "And ye shall serve the Lord your God . . . and I will take sickness away from the midst of thee." Exodus 23:25.

God gave health rules because He knows what is best for the human body which He, Himself, made. Automobile manufacturers place an "operations manual" in the glove compartment of each new car, because they know what is best for their product. God, who made our bodies, also has an "operations manual." It is the Holy Bible. Ignoring God's "operations manual" results in disease, twisted thinking, and burnt-out lives just as abusing a car (against the manufacturer's counsel) results in serious car trouble. Following God's rules results in "saving health" (Psalm 67:2) and more "abundant" life (John 10:10). These great health laws are a wall or fence to keep us out of the diseases of Satan.

Do God's health rules have anything to do with eating and drinking?

"Eat ye that which is good." Isaiah 55:2. "Whether therefore ye eat, or drink, or whatsoever ye do, do all to the glory of God." 1 Corinthians 10:31.

A Christian will eat and drink differently,—all to the glory of God, using only "that which is good." If God says a thing is not fit to eat, He must have a good reason. He is not a harsh dictator, but a loving Father. All His counsel is for our good always. The Bible promises that "no good thing will He withhold from them that walk uprightly." Psalm 84:11. So if God withholds a thing from us, it is because it is not good.

What did God give man to eat when He created him and provided a perfect diet?

"And God said, Behold, I have given you every herb bearing seed . . . and every tree . . . yielding seed." "Of every tree of the garden thou mayest freely eat." "And thou shalt eat the herb of the field." Genesis 1:29; 2:16; 3:18. The diet

God gave to man in the beginning was fruit, grains and nuts. Vegetables were also added a bit later.

What items are specifically mentioned by God as being unclean or forbidden?

In Leviticus 11 and Deuteronomy 14, God clearly points out the following groups as being unclean. Read both chapters in full.

(1) All animals which do not have a split hoof and chew cud. Deuteronomy 14:6.
(2) All fish and water creatures that do not have both fins and scales. Deuteronomy 14:9.
(3) All birds of prey, carrion eaters and fish eaters. Leviticus 11:13-20.
(4) Most "creeping things" or invertebrates are unclean. Leviticus 11:21-47.

According to God's rules, the following are unclean and are not to be eaten: the hog, the squirrel, the rabbit, the catfish, the lamprey eel, lobsters, clams, shrimps (in fact, all "seafood") and frogs.

What is the Lord's attitude toward intoxicating beverages?

"Wine is a mocker, strong drink is raging: and whosoever is deceived thereby is not wise." Proverbs 20:1. "Look not upon the wine when it is red, when it giveth his colour in the cup, when it moveth itself aright. At last it biteth like a serpent, and stingeth like an adder." Proverbs 23:31, 32. "Nor thieves . . . nor drunkards . . . shall inherit the kingdom of God." 1 Corinthians 6:10.

Despite the subtle allurement of the liquour advertisements, common sense tells us that intoxicants are ruinous. Moreover, no drunkard can enter heaven.

Does the Bible condemn the use of tobacco?

Yes, following are seven Bible reasons why the use of tobacco is displeasing to God:

(1) It contains nicotine, a deadly poison. God says He will destroy those who use "poisonous herbs." See Deuteronomy 29:17-19. Note margin for verse 18.

(2) Nicotine is a narcotic that enslaves a man. Whoever and whatever we obey, we serve. Romans 6:16. Tobacco users are servants of nicotine.

(3) The use of tobacco injures health and defiles the body, making it unfit as a dwelling place for the Holy Spirit. 1 Corinthians 3:16, 17.

(4) The use of tobacco wastes money. "Wherefore do ye spend money for that which is not bread?" Isaiah 55:2.

(5) Tobacco using is a fleshly lust. "Abstain from fleshly lusts, which war against the soul." 1 Peter 2:11. The use of tobacco never draws anyone closer to Christ.

(6) The tobacco habit is unclean. "Come out from among them, and be ye separate, saith the Lord, and touch not the unclean thing; and I will receive you." 2 Corinthians 6:17.

(7) The use of tobacco shortens life. Recent scientific findings establish the fact that the use of tobacco often shortens the life span by as much as one third. This breaks God's command against killing (Exodus 20:13). Even though it is slow murder, it is still murder. One of the best ways to postpone your funeral is to quit using tobacco.

What are some simple, yet very important health laws found in the Bible?

Here are eleven Bible health rules. Read the texts from your Bible.

(1) Eat your meals at regular intervals and do not use animal "fat" or blood. Ecclesiastes 10:17; Leviticus 3:17. Recent scientific studies have established the fact that most heart attacks result from a high cholesterol level in the blood and that the use of fats is largely responsible for this high level.

(2) Don't over-eat. Proverbs 32:2. In Luke 21:34 Christ specifically warns against "surfeiting" in the last days. Overeating or surfeiting is responsible for many degenerative diseases.

(3) Don't harbor envy or hold grudges. Proverbs 14:30; Matthew 5:23, 24.

(4) Maintain a cheerful, happy disposition. Proverbs 17:22; 23:7. Many diseases from which men suffer are a result of mental depression. A cheerful, happy disposition imparts health and prolongs life.

(5) Put full trust in the Lord. Proverbs 19:23; 4:20, 22.

(6) Balance work and exercise with sleep and rest. Exodus 20:9, 10; Ecclesiastes 5:12; Genesis 3:19; Proverbs 127:2; Ecclesiastes 2:23.

(7) Keep your body clean. "Be ye clean." Isaiah 52:11.

(8) Be temperate in all things. 1 Corinthians 9:25; Philippians 4:5.

(9) Avoid all stimulants. Medical science has established the fact that tea, coffee, and cola drinks, which contain the addictive drug caffeine and other harmful ingredients, are all positively damaging to the human body.

(10) Make mealtime a happy time. Ecclesiastes 3:13. Unhappy scenes at mealtime hinder digestion. Avoid them.

(11) Help those who are in need. Isaiah 58:6-8. This is too plain to misunderstand: when we help the poor, sick and needy, we increase our own health.

What will not be permitted to enter God's kingdom?

"There shall in no wise enter into it anything that defileth." Revelation 21:27. Nothing defiling or unclean will get there. All filthy habits defile a person. We are admonished to "clean ourselves from all filthiness of the flesh." 2 Corinthians 7:1. In the light of the second coming of Christ, every Christian will purify his life. 1 John 3:3.

How can a person gain the victory over bad habits?

"As many as received Him, to them gave he power to become the sons of God." John 1:12. "I can do all things through Christ which strengtheneth me." Philippians 4:13. Take all these things to Christ and lay them at His feet. He will give you the power you need to break any evil and become a son or daughter of God (Ezekiel 11:18-20). How thrilling and heartwarming it is to know that "with God all things are possible" (Mark 10:27). And Jesus says, "Him that cometh to me I will in no wise cast out" (John 6:37).

"Beloved, I wish above all things that thou mayest prosper and be in health, even as thy soul prospereth."

3 John 2

Objections to the Saturday Sabbath

By Manny P. Mullaneda

A lie told many times is easily accepted as truth especially if it has been around a long time.

Take the case of the spider. In 350 B. C. Aristotle, the great Greek Philosopher said that the spider has six legs, and this was accepted as truth for the next 2,000 years. But when Lamarck, the outstanding biologist spent time to carefully count the legs of the spider, he found out that there are exactly eight legs! The myth or lie was destroyed because Lamarck bothered to count.

Did you bother to find out which really is the true Bible Sabbath? Is it Sunday? Saturday" or any other day? The acceptance of religious myth could have life or death consequences. It's therefore important to be able to distinguish between lie and truth. But where do we get the fact? It's not what one thinks that makes the fact, but it is what God says. The Bible is the final authority. When tempted by Satan, Jesus answered: "It is written!"

Before we delve deeper on the objections let's cite some facts about the 7th-day Sabbath which religious groups accept and agree:

- That the 7th—day sabbath is one of the Ten Commandants of God which says: "Remember the Sabbath day to keep it holy. Six days shall you all labor and do all your work: But the seventh day is the sabbath of the Lord your God: in it you shall not do any work, you, nor your son, nor your daughter, your manservant, nor maidservant, nor your cattle, nor your stranger that is within your gates: For in six days the Lord made heaven, and earth, the sea, and all that in them is, and rested the seventh day: therefore the Lord blessed and hallowed it." (Exodus 20:8-11).

- That Saturday is the seventh day of the week (See the meaning of Saturday in the dictionary).
- That sabbath means day of worship and rest from work.

Objection: The New Testament is silent as to any command to keep the Sabbath.

Answer: Jesus commanded by saying: The sabbath was made for man" (Mark 2:27-28). You are a man, and I am a man. What Jesus is saying here is: "I made the Sabbath for you - man!" What further command do you want?

Objection: The sabbath was given only to the Jews.

Answer: Why don't we use the language of the Bible and call the 4th commandment "The Sabbath of the Lord"? (Exodus 20:10). "The Sabbath was made for man" (Mark 2:27). The sabbath was made and given to man 2,500 years before the existence of Jew. (Genesis 2:1-3).

Objection: The New Testament teach that the disciples worshiped on the first day of the week.

Answer: The first day of the week is mentioned only 8 times in the entire New Testament and six of these refer to the same day. Matthew 28:1 "After the Sabbath, at dawn on the first day of the week, Mary Magdalene and the other Mary went to look at the tomb". Other similar passages are recorded in Mark 16:2; Mark 16:9; Luke 24:1; and John 20:1. These five texts simply state the historical fact that Jesus rose from the dead on the first day of the week. They don't mention any worship made on that day. Now let's closely examine the remaining 3 texts in detail: John 20:19 - "On the evening of that first day of the week, when the disciples were together, with the doors locked for fear of the Jews, Jesus came and stood among them and said, "Peace be with you!"

This passage says that the disciples assembled on the first day of the week not to worship, but "for fear of the Jews." They just witnessed how Jesus was nailed on the cross and died. No wonder the doors were locked. Then Jesus appeared to announce that He has risen from the grave. He did not command to worship on the first day.

I Corinthian 16:2 - "On the first day of every week, each one of you should set aside a sum of money in keeping with his income, saving it up, so that when I come no collections will have to be made.

"Paul was promoting a special project in behalf of the needy believers in Jerusalem (verse 8), Thus he suggested that Corinthian Christians set aside a specific portion of their income for poor believers at Jerusalem on the first day of each week. The reason for this was on Friday afternoon believers would close their shops and prepare for the sabbath which starts at sunset. Then on Sunday morning they would review the previous week's business activity. Paul was simply asking them to set some money aside so that when he arrived the gift would be ready to be taken to Jerusalem. The phrase "set aside" means literally "by himself," in the original Greek manuscript. It is also equivalent to the English "at home" and has no reference to any church meeting." (The Almost Forgotten Day by Mark A. Finley, p. 167).

Acts 20:7 - "On the first day of the week we come together to break bread. Paul spoke to the people and, because he intended to leave the next day, kept on talking until midnight."

This first day of the week gathering happened on Saturday night. The sabbath observance is from sunset of Friday to sunset of Saturday. So the dark part of Saturday night is already counted as first day of the week. (Leviticus 23:32). Paul preached until midnight. He walked 19 miles to Assos the next day (Sunday). This does not make Sunday as sabbath.

Objection: Did Jesus and His disciples keep the Sabbath?

Answer: Jesus, as His custom went to church every 7th-day Sabbath (Luke 4:16). Virgin Mary and Mary Magdalene when Jesus was buried on Friday prepared spices and ointment, and the next day (Saturday Sabbath) they rested according to the commandment (Luke 23:54-56). Apostle Paul made it his custom to go to church and keep the Sabbath (Acts 17:1, 2:18:1-4). The redeemed in heaven shall worship the Lord every Sabbath (Isaiah 66:23).

Objection: "Man is saved by grace through faith. So he can't earn salvation by keeping the Sabbath.

Answer: It is true that man can't earn salvation by keeping the Sabbath or the law. But he keeps the Sabbath as the result of his faith and love for Jesus who said: "If you love me, keep my commandments."

"God's purpose for us on the Sabbath are: 1. He desires that the sabbath be a day of spiritual worship and praise. (Exodus 20:8-11; Leviticus 23:2). 2. He has designed the Sabbath to be a day of physical rest. 3. God has intended for the Sabbath to be a day of fellowship with one another, especially our families.

The Bible declares that all purchases should be made before the Sabbath (Nehemiah 13: 15-18). All secular matters/activities should be finished before the Sabbath begins. (Isaiah 58:13). God has designed the Sabbath to be the happiest day of our week. We can look forward to each Sabbath as a special time for joy and fellowship with Jesus Himself". (The Almost Forgotten Day, by Mark A. Finley).

"Be ready always to give an answer to every man that asks you a reason of the hope that is in you with meekness and fear." (I Peter 3:15).

Many thinking people shoot questions and objections on doctrines. Valid objections from sincere truth-seekers if properly handled and answered may turn into interest in knowing more about Bible truth. So "be ready always to give an answer."

The seventh-day (Saturday) sabbath is the mark or sign between God and His people. "Moreover also I gave them my sabbaths, to be a sign between me and them, that they might know that I am the Lord that sanctify them." (Ezekiel 20:12).

Objection: Since Jesus declared that the greatest of all the commandments is love, we don't have to be concerned with keeping the Ten Commandments including the sabbath as long as we love God and our neighbors.

Answer: A lawyer asked Jesus a question: "Master, which is the great commandment in the law? Jesus said to him, Love the Lord with all your heart and with all your soul and with all your mind. This is the first and the greatest commandment. And the second is like it: Love your neighbor as yourself. All the law and the prophets hang on these two commandments (Matthew 22:37-40).

It is a mistake to think and believe that these are new laws to replace the Ten Commandments. Jesus was simply quoting directly from Deuteronomy 6:5 of the Old Testament which says: "Love the Lord your God with all your heart and with all your soul and with all your strength." Then Leviticus 19:18 says: "... Love your neighbor as yourself." God using His own fingers wrote the 10 commandments in two tables of stones. The first table (1-4 commandments) refers to Love to God such as: You shall have no other gods ... you shall not take the name of the Lord your God in vain, remember the sabbath day to keep it holy. While the second table (5-10 commandments) refers to love to man. If you love your neighbor, you do not steal, kill, commit adultery, bear false witnesses..."

Objection: The apostle John calls Sunday the Lord's day and declares that he was "in the spirit on the Lord's day." This proves that Sunday is the sacred weekly rest-day of the Christian church. (Read Revelation 1:10).

Answer: The Lord's day is not Sunday as some people think. Christ is the "Lord of the Sabbath" (Mark 2:27). Therefore the sabbath (7th-day) is the Lord's day.

Objection: It makes no difference which day to keep. God is not particular.

Answer: The text used is Romans 14:5: "One man esteems one day above another: another esteems everyday alike. Let every man be fully persuaded in his own mind. He that regards the day, regards it to the Lord; and he that regards not the day, to the Lord he does not regard it. He that eats, eats to the Lord, for he gives God thanks; and he that eats not, to the Lord he eats not, and gives God thanks."

A closer look at the text reveal that it does not talk about sabbath or worship. The issue here is on days of fasting. Take note of the 'words "eats" and "eats not" (abstaining from food or fasting). Some of the Jewish Christians during Paul's days fasted on certain days, and those who didn't fast on these days were looked down. They judged others by their own standard which caused division in the church. What Paul stressed was: "If you want to fast on certain days, fine, but don't judge everybody else by your own choice." The discussion is a matter of human opinion rather than a divine command. Another point to consider is the preceding text (Romans 14:1-3 which was a matter of opinion on whether to eat or not to eat meat offered to the idols worshiped by the sellers in the market. All these have nothing to do with sabbath-keeping.

God is particular. Take the case of Naaman who was instructed to dip into Jordan river seven times for the healing of leprosy. He was not healed at the count of 5 or 6. But immediately after the count of seven, leprosy was gone. When God says 7th day, it's not the first, second or third.

Objection: The law of God ended, therefore we do not have to keep the sabbath.

Answer: The verse used is Romans 10:4: "For Christ is the end of the law for righteousness to every one that believes." But what about the verse in James which says: "Ye have heard of the patience of Job, and have seen the end of the Lord." James 5:11 Did this mean the Lord came to an end? And that he stopped existing? Of course we know that God has not stopped functioning. So you now think of another meaning of "end" as the dictionary defines as "the purpose of an action or existence, or the objective." If someone says: "We work toward a common end" meaning common objective." Therefore the passage "For Christ is the end of the law" means Christ is the objective of the law. "In other words, the law cannot save a person, but it shuts him up under condemnation until Christ is the only way of escape. Christ is the end or object of the law." (Another Look at the Christian Sabbath, by J. L. Tucker p. 81.)

Objection: We now kept Sunday sabbath in honor of Christ's resurrection.

Answer: Those who worship on Sunday because Jesus rose from the dead on that day do so without any command from God. So they don't have to worry and fear that they sin if they don't keep it. Where there's no law, there is no sin because sin is the transgression of the law. To commemorate Christ's resurrection, the Bible specifies baptism (not Sunday) as an emblem. Romans 6:4,5 says: "We were therefore buried with him through baptism unto death in order that just as Christ was raised from the dead through the glory of the Father, we too may live a new life. If we have been united with him like this in his death, will certainly also be united with him in his resurrection." The Bible baptism is dipping into a river or water symbolizing burial of sinful self in the watery grave, then the believer rises up as being resurrected to new life.

Objection: In Hosea 2:11 God said He shall cause the sabbath to stop. So there's no need to keep it now.

Answer: The text says: "I will also cause all her mirth to cease, her feast day, her new moons, and her sabbath." Notice the word "her" sabbath.

To avoid confusion, let's differentiate some kinds' of sabbaths in the Bible such as: a) Her sabbath (rest of the land every 7th year). "Six years you shall sow your field, and six years you shall prune your vineyard, and gather in the fruit thereof. But in the seventh year shall be a sabbath or rest unto the land, a sabbath for the Lord: you shall neither sow your field, nor prune your vineyard." Then shall the land enjoy her sabbath. (Leviticus 25:2,4; Lev. 26:34). b) Your sabbath (yearly). Leviticus 23:27, 32: "It shall be a sabbath of rest, and you shall afflict your souls: in the ninth day of the (seventh) month at sunset, from sunset to sunset shall you celebrate your sabbath." Look, this sabbath does not necessarily fall on the 7th day of the week. It's a yearly sabbath, c) My sabbath (7th day weekly sabbath in the Ten Commandments). "Moreover also I gave them my sabbaths to be a sign between me and them, that they might know that I am the Lord that sanctify them." (Ezekiel 20:12;) Also called "the sabbath of the Lord." (Exodus 20:8-10).

What ceased in Hosea 2:11 was her sabbath (rest of the land every 7th year. Also abolished when Jesus was nailed on the cross, were the sabbaths contained in the handwriting of ordinances, which ended when Jesus "Blotting out the handwriting of ordinances that was against us, which was contrary to us and took it out of the way, nailing it to his cross; Let no man therefore judge you in meat, or drink, or in respect of a holiday, or of the new moon, or of the sabbath days; which are a shadow of things to come; but the body is of Christ." (Colossians 2:14,16). The sabbath days that were abolished include the yearly sabbaths. But the seventh-day of the week (My sabbath) being part of the Ten Commandments continues to be remembered and kept even in heaven. (Isaiah 66:22, 23).

"For as the new heavens and the new earth, which I will make, shall remain before me, saith the Lord, so shall your seed and your name remain. And it shall come to pass, that from one new moon to another, and from one sabbath to another, shall all flesh come to worship before me, saith the Lord."

Your Day In Court

A college student was awakened about five o'clock one morning by a knocking on his door. A policeman entered his bedroom and handed him a summons to court. The police asked the student to go as a witness, but the student didn't want to go. He soon learned, however, that when a witness is summoned by the court, he must go. It is not a matter of whether he wants to go or likes to go or has time to go, he *must* go.

The Bible tells us that we must all appear before the judgment seat of Christ. There is no way to escape our day in court! The question we must answer is, are we ready to stand before the bar of justice and hear the verdict?

More than 2,500 years ago, Belshazzar, a Babylonian king, with a thousand of his government officials, feasted and amused themselves in a beautiful dining hall. They all felt perfectly secure in the great capital city of Babylon. They drank wine, feasted and rejoiced in their power and wealth. The king and his nobles not only felt superior in every way to other nations, but even showed contempt to the God of heaven. The king ordered his servants to bring out the golden vessels which his armies had stolen from the holy temple in Jerusalem. They then drank wine from these sacred cups until they were thoroughly intoxicated.

God took notice of this defiance on the part of Belshazzar. Suddenly Belshazzar and his officials were brought to their senses. There was a movement on the palace wall and a bloodless hand wrote a message of judgment. It was a message of doom from God.

The Bible states (Daniel 5) that when Belshazzar saw this hand writing he was so fearful that "his knees smote one against another." He summoned the prophet Daniel. Daniel read the message to the king. Belshazzar was found guilty of rebellion against God. Belshazzar not only lost his life and kingdom on earth, he was unprepared and will also lose eternal life and a part in God's kingdom.

We all have this appointment with God.

How many of us will have to appear before the judgment seat of Christ?

"For we must all appear before the judgment seat of Christ; that every one may receive the things *done* in *his* body, according to that he hath done, whether *it be* good or bad." 2 Corinthians 5:10.

To whom will man have to give an account in that day?

"So then every one of us shall give account of himself to God." Romans 14:12.

With whom will this investigative judgment begin?

"For the time *is come* that judgment must begin at the house of God: and if *it* first *begin* at us, what shall the end *be* of them that obey not the gospel of God?" 1 Peter 4:17.

In what words does the Bible tell that there is a definite time for the judgment?

"Because he hath appointed a day, in the which he will judge the world in righteousness by *that* man whom he hath ordained; *whereof* he hath given assurance unto all *men,* in that he hath raised him from the dead." Acts 17:31.

What message is to be proclaimed to all the world announcing the beginning of this judgment?

"And I saw another angel fly in the midst of heaven, having the everlasting gospel to preach unto them that dwell on the earth, and to every nation, and kindred, and tongue, and people, saying with a loud voice, Fear God, and give glory to him; for the hour of His judgment is come: and worship him that made heaven, and earth, and the sea, and the fountains of waters." Revelation 14:6, 7.

What records are used as evidence?

"And I saw a great white throne, and him that sat on it, from whose face the earth and the heaven fled away; and there was found no place for them. And I saw the dead, small and great, stand before God; and the books were opened, which is *the book* of life: and the dead were judged out of those things which were written in the books, according to their works." Revelation 20:11, 12.

Whom does Daniel say presides at the judgment?

"I beheld till the thrones were cast down, and the Ancient of days did sit, whose garment was white as snow, and the hair of his head like the pure wool: his throne *was like* the fiery flame, *and* his wheels *as* burning fire. A fiery stream issued and came forth from before him: thousand and thousands ministered unto him, and ten thousand times ten thousand stood before him: the judgment was set, and the books were opened." Daniel 7:9, 10.

NOTE: The Ancient of Days is God the Father, whom the Son of God approaches as our Advocate (verse 13). "Cast down" in verse 9 means "placed"—see marginal reading.

How much of what we have done will be known in that day?

"Let us hear the conclusion of the whole matter: Fear God, and keep his commandments: for this *is* the whole *duty* of man. For God shall bring every work into judgment, with every secret thing, whether it be good, or whether *it be* evil." Ecclesiastes 12:13, 14.

What did Christ say about our words?

"But I say unto you, That every idle word that men shall speak, they shall give account thereof in the day of judgment. For by thy words thou shalt be justified, and by thy words thou shalt be condemned." Matthew 12:36, 37.

What book contains the records of those who follow the Lord?

"Then they that feared the Lord spake often one to another: and the Lord hearkened, and heard it, and a book of remembrance was written before him for them that feared the Lord, and that thought upon his name." Malachi 3:16.

In what book are the names recorded of those who have accepted Christ?

"And I intreat thee also, true yokefellow, help those women which laboured with me in the gospel, with Clement also, and *with* other my fellow labourers, whose names *are* in the book of life." Philippians 4:3.

What happens to the name of one who once confessed Christ but afterwards turned to a life of sin?

"And Moses returned unto the Lord, and said, Oh, this people have sinned a great sin, and have made them gods of gold. Yet now, if thou wilt forgive their sin—; and if not, blot me, I pray thee, out of thy book which thou hast written. And the Lord said unto Moses, Whosoever hath sinned against me, him will I blot out of my book." Exodus 32:31-33.

What promise is given to the overcomer?

"He that overcometh, the same shall be clothed in white raiment; and I will not blot out his name out of the book of life, but I will confess his name before my Father, and before his angels." Revelation 3:5.

What law will be the standard of the judgment?

"For whosoever shall keep the whole law, and yet offend in one *point,* he is guilty of all. For he that said, Do not commit adultery, said also, Do not kill. Now if thou commit no adultery, yet if thou kill, thou art become a transgressor of the law. So speak ye, and so do, as they that shall be judged by the law of liberty." James 2:10-12.

What does Christ do for us in the judgment?

"Wherefore he is able also to save them to the uttermost that come unto God by him, seeing he ever liveth to make intercession for them." Hebrews 7:25.

If we sin, what hope is held out to us?

"My little children, these things write I unto you, that ye sin not. And if any man sin, we have an advocate with the Father, Jesus Christ the righteous: And he is the propitiation for our sins: and not for ours only, but also for *the sins of* the whole world." 1 John 2:1, 2.

In Paul's day the judgment was still future. Acts 24:25. When Christ comes "His reward is with Him," (see Revelation 22:12) that is, the judgment is over. We are now in the judgment hour, according to the Bible. Daniel 8:14; Revelation 14:7. The cases of those who have accepted Christ are being examined. Those who have become overcomers through His power will be cleansed from all their sins.

Those who have made a profession, but by their lives have denied their Lord, will have their names removed from the book of life. There are many who have a form of godliness, but by their acts they deny the power of God in their lives. These will not enter the eternal city. Their works testify that they were Christians only in name. Christ describes this group of people in Matthew 7:21-23. "Not everyone that saith unto Me, Lord, Lord, shall enter into the kingdom of heaven; but he that doeth the will of My Father which is in heaven. Many will say to Me in that day, Lord, Lord, have we not prophesied in Thy name? and in Thy name have cast out devils? and in Thy name done many wonderful works? And then will I profess unto them, I never knew you: depart from Me, ye that work iniquity."

The righteous, on the other hand, show by the fruitage of their lives that the Lord rules them. The life that they now live, they live by the power that God imparts to them through the indwelling of Christ. If we are Christ's and He is our Advocate in the judgment day, the record of His perfect life of obedience will be applied to our record in heaven. The guilt of our sins and mistakes was borne by Him upon the cross of Calvary. We will stand before God in that day as though we had never sinned. Gone will be the record of our mistakes. They will be forgiven and blotted out. Why should we worry about the past or the future when we may have forgiveness today?

The Saviour stands ready to plead your case. He wants to be your Advocate. Will you not place your case in His hands?

"For God shall bring every work into judgment, with every secret thing, whether it be good, or whether it be evil."

Ecclesiastes 12:14

Does Christ Have A Church Today?

Pilot Tan could not believe his instruments. Flying through the clouds, he felt sure his plane was banking to the left. But according to the horizon line on his instrument panel, he was tipped to the right! Tan remembered the warning his flight instructor had given about vertigo—the deadly dizziness that deceives pilots into thinking *up* is *down*. Still he was sure he was right. "Straightening" the plane out he radioed that his instruments were out of order. That was the last message the control tower heard from him. The next day the wreckage of his plane was found on a hillside.

What went wrong with Pilot Tan? He believed his feelings instead of his instruments. Many people say, "It doesn't make any difference what you believe, as long as you are sincere." But sincerity is not enough. We must be right. We must follow the guide God has given us—the Holy Bible. We must be certain that we accept Bible truths, not error.

Every teaching comes either from the Source of truth or from the originator of error. We cannot safely follow our feelings, for God has told us, "There is a way that seemeth right unto a man, but the end thereof are the ways of death." Proverbs 16:25. We must be certain that we accept Bible truth not error.

Has God given us any way of knowing what is truth? Is there any way to identify the true church? How can I tell what to do and believe? God has not left us in darkness. Foreseeing this very need He gave us a prophecy that answers the question. Let us study it now.

What is the true church called in the Bible?

"But if I tarry long, that thou mayest know how thou oughtest to behave thyself in the house of God, which is the church of the living God, the pillar and ground of the truth." 1 Timothy 3:15.

NOTE: *God's true church in every age will be the depository of truth. His church teaches the truth.*

PLEASE READ REVELATION 12 BEFORE YOU PROCEED.

To whom does God compare the daughter of Zion?

"I have likened the daughter of Zion to a comely and delicate *woman*." Jeremiah 6:2.

Who is Zion?

"And I have put my words in thy mouth, and I have covered thee in the shadow of mine hand, that I may plant the heavens, and lay the foundations of the earth, and say unto Zion, Thou *art* my people." Isaiah 51:16.

NOTE: God has used the symbol of a pure woman to represent His people or His church. Paul describes the church of Corinth as a chaste virgin. 2 Corinthians 11.2. The woman of Revelation 12:1 is God's way of picturing the Christian church in its battle with Satan.

Who is represented by the great red dragon?

"And there was war in heaven: Michael and his angels fought against the dragon; and the dragon fought and his angels, and prevailed not; neither was their place found any more in heaven. And the great dragon was cast out, that old serpent, called the Devil, and Satan, which deceiveth the whole world: he was cast out into the earth, and his angels were cast out with him." Revelation 12:7-9.

Under what symbol is Christ pictured in this prophecy?

"And she brought forth a man child, who was to rule all nations with a rod of iron: and her child was caught up unto God, and *to* his throne." Revelation 12:5.

How did the devil try to destroy Christ as soon as He was born?

"And there appeared another wonder in heaven; and behold a great red dragon, having seven heads and ten horns, and seven crowns upon his heads. And his tail drew the third part of the stars of heaven, and did cast them to the earth: and the dragon stood before the woman which was ready to be delivered for to devour her child as soon as it was born." Revelation 12:3, 4.

"Now when Jesus was born in Bethlehem of Judaea in the days of Herod the king, behold, there came wise men from the east to Jerusalem, saying, Where is he that is born King of the Jews? for we have seen his star in the east, and are come to worship him. When Herod the king had heard *these things,* he was troubled, and all Jerusalem with him, And when he had gathered all the chief priests and scribes of the people together, he demanded of them where Christ should be born. And they said unto him, in Bethlehem of Judaea: for thus it is written by the prophet, And thou Bethlehem, in the land of Juda, art not the least among the princes of Juda: for out of thee shall come a Governor, that shall rule my people Israel. Then Herod, when he had privily called the wise men, enquired of them diligently what time the star appeared. And he sent them to Bethlehem, and said, Go and search diligently for the young child; and when ye have found *him,* bring me word again, that I may come and worship him also. When they had heard the king, they departed; and, lo, the star, which they saw in the east, went before them, till it came and stood over where the young child was. When they saw the star, they rejoiced with exceeding great joy. And when they were come into the house, they saw the young child with Mary his mother, and fell down, and worshipped him: and when they had opened their treasures, they presented unto him gifts; gold, and frankincense, and myrrh. And being warned of God in a dream that they should not return to Herod, they departed into their own country another way.

And when they were departed, behold, the angel of the Lord appeareth to Joseph in a dream, saying, Arise, and take the young child and his mother, and flee into Egypt, and be thou there until I bring thee word: for Herod will seek the young child to destroy him. When he arose, he took the young child and his mother, by night, and departed into Egypt: and was there until the death of Herod: that it might be fulfilled which was spoken of the Lord by the prophet, saying, Out of Egypt have I called my son. Then Herod, when he saw that he was mocked of the wise men, was exceeding wroth, and sent forth, and slew all the children that were in Bethlehem, and in all the coasts thereof, from two years old and under, according to the time which he had diligently enquired of the wise men." Matthew 2:1-16.

As the devil realizes that his days are numbered, what does he do to the woman who represents the church?

"And when the dragon saw that he was cast unto the earth, he persecuted the woman which brought forth the man *child*. And to the woman were given two wings of a great eagle, that she might fly into the wilderness, into her place, where she is nourished for a time, and times, and half a time, from the face of the serpent." Revelation 12:13, 14.

Where did the woman (church) flee to escape the persecution which lasted 1260 years?

"And the woman fled into the wilderness, where she hath a place prepared of God, that they should feed her there a thousand two hundred *and* threescore days. . . . And to the woman were given two wings of a great eagle, that she might fly into the wilderness, into her place, where she is nourished for a time, and times, and half a time, from the face of the serpent." Revelation 12:6, 14.

NOTE: The prophetic time period here mentioned represents 1260 literal years. Ezekiel 4:6 provides the prophetic rule that one day of prophetic time equals one literal year. Prophetic interpretation accepts this principle that a symbolic day in Bible prophecy represents a literal year.

Against what part of the true church does the devil especially direct his wrath and final warfare?

"And the dragon was wroth with the woman, and went to make war with the remnant of her seed, which keep the commandments of God, and have the testimony of Jesus Christ." Revelation 12:17.

NOTE: The "remnant" is the last part. Just as a remnant of a bolt of cloth is the last part of that roll, so the remnant of God's church is the last portion of His church on earth.

What are the two special identification marks of the remnant, or last part, of the true church?

"And the dragon was wroth with the woman, and went to make war with the remnant of her seed, which keep the commandments of God, and have the testimony of Jesus Christ." Revelation 12:17.

NOTE: Revelation 19:10 says that the "testimony of Jesus is the spirit of prophecy."

Which commandment of God does nearly the whole Christian world ignore?

"Remember the sabbath day, to keep it holy. Six days shalt thou labour, and do all thy work: But the seventh day *is* the sabbath of the Lord thy God: *in it* thou shalt not do any work, thou, nor thy son, nor thy daughter, thy manservant, nor thy maidservant, nor thy cattle, nor thy stranger that *is* within thy gates: For *in* six days the Lord made heaven and earth, the sea, and all that in them , and rested the seventh day: wherefore the Lord blessed the sabbath day, and hallowed it." Exodus 20:8-11.

NOTE: *In order to be the true church which keeps all the commandments of God, that church must keep God's Sabbath day.*

What threefold message will be proclaimed in all the world by this church?

"And I saw another angel fly in the midst of heaven, having the everlasting gospel to preach unto them that dwell on the earth, and to every nation, and kindred, and tongue, and people, saying with a loud voice, Fear God, and give glory to him; for the hour of his judgment is come: and worship him that made heaven, and earth, and the sea, and the fountains of waters. And there followed another angel, saying, Babylon is fallen, is fallen, that great city, because she made all nations drink of the wine of the wrath of her fornication. And the third angel followed them, saying with a loud voice, If any man worship the beast and his image, and receive *his* mark in his forehead, or in his hand, the same shall drink of the wine of the wrath of God, which is poured out without mixture into the cup of his indignation; and he shall be tormented with fire and brimstone in the presence of the holy angels, and in the presence of the Lamb: And the smoke of their torment 'ascendeth up for ever and ever: and they have no rest day nor night, who worship the beast and his image, and whosoever receiveth the mark of his name. Here is the patience of the saints: here *are* they that keep the commandments of God, and the faith of Jesus." Revelation 14:6-12.

How does God describe the people who are called out by this threefold message and who prepare for the coming of Christ?

"Here is the patience of the saints: here *are* they that keep the commandments of God, and the faith of Jesus. And I heard a voice from heaven saying unto me, Write, Blessed *are* the dead which die in the Lord from henceforth: Yes, saith the Spirit, that they may rest from their labours; and their works do follow them. And I looked, and behold a white cloud, and upon the cloud *one* sat like unto the Son of man, having on his head a golden crown, and in his hand a sharp sickle." Revelation 14:12-14.

What call does God make to His people who are in the false or confused religious bodies of the world today?

"And after these things I saw another angel come down from heaven, having great power; and the earth was lightened with his glory. And he cried mightily with a strong voice, saying, Babylon the great is fallen, is fallen, and is become the habitation of devils, and the hold of every foul spirit, and a cage of every unclean and hateful bird. For all nations have drunk of the wine of the wrath of her fornication, and the kings of the earth have committed fornication with her, and the merchants of the earth are waxed rich through the abundance of her delicacies. And I heard another voice from heaven, saying, Come out of her, my people, that ye be not partakers of her sins, and that ye receive not of her plagues." Revelation 18:1-4.

Speaking of His true people, it is more than coincidence that in two different places in the book of Revelation God says of them, they "keep the commandments of God." In this age of spiritual confusion, many religious leaders teach that God does not want His followers to keep His commandments. They go so far as to assert that the commandments of God have been abolished by the death of Christ. We see from this prophecy that God, by His divine foresight, knew what was going to be taught today. He pictures His people as those who keep His commandments. Those who carry His last gospel message to the world are described as those who are obedient to Him. They obey Him because they love Him supremely, and their obedience is a manifestation of this love.

In finding the true church as described in Revelation, we must find a church which keeps all of God's commandments, which surely includes the Sabbath. It also is a Christian church, for it accepts "the faith of Jesus." This church must have the gift of prophecy in its midst, and it must be working in all of the world giving the threefold gospel message of Revelation 14. Look about you today, and you will find only one church that has all of God's identifying marks of the true church. When you find this church, you will want to unite with it and share in the joy of giving the gospel to all the world.

"Here is the patience of the saints: here are they that keep the commandments of God, and the faith of Jesus."

Revelation 14:12

Why Should I Be Baptized?

Many years ago in the land of Syria there lived a man by the name of Naaman. We are not told very much about him, but we do know that he was the commander of the Syrian army and that one day he discovered that he had leprosy. Today a person can be cured of leprosy, but in those days the discovery that a person had this disease meant only one thing—a slow, lingering death.

Evidently Naaman was a very good man and a valuable soldier because the King of Syria inquired about a cure for this servant. A little Hebrew maid, who was a servant in the home of Naaman, heard of her master's plight and declared that God's prophet, Elisha, could heal him if he went up to Samaria.

Like most people who have some deadly disease, Naaman was willing to try anything. When he arrived with a request for his healing from the King of Syria, the King of Israel was concerned about this unusual request, Elisha, however, sent word that God would take care of the problem. When Naaman came to the house of Elisha, the prophet did not even meet him at the door. Elisha just sent his servant out with a message that if Naaman wanted to be healed, he merely had to go and wash seven times in the Jordan River.

At first Naaman was furious and refused to do this, but after a talk with his wise servants, he obeyed and washed seven times in the Jordan. The Bible tells us of the results of his trusting God and doing what he had been told. It states, "And his flesh came again like unto the flesh of a little child, and he was clean." 2 Kings 5:14. He was cleansed because he had faith and obeyed the instructions of God given through His prophet, Elisha.

There were no secret healing substances in the water of that river. Naaman's dipping seven times was merely his way of demonstrating his faith in the God of Israel. It was God that cleansed and healed him. Many of us are afflicted with spiritual leprosy or sin, and we need to be cleansed from all these sins. Let us discover in God's Word how we can be cleansed.

How many different baptisms are recognized in the Bible?
"One Lord, one faith, one baptism." Ephesians 4:5.

What were the final instructions given by Christ to His disciples?

"Go ye therefore, and teach all nations, baptizing them in the name of the Father, and of the Son, and of the Holy Ghost: teaching them to observe all things whatsoever I have commanded you: and, lo, I am with you alway, *even* unto the end of the world Amen." Matthew 28:19, 20.

Who originated the modern form of baptism?

"In those days came John the Baptist, preaching in the wilderness of Judaea, and saying, Repent ye: for the kingdom of heaven is at hand. For this is he that was spoken of by the prophet Esaias, saying, The voice of one crying in the wilderness, Prepare ye the way of the Lord, make his paths straight. And the same John had his raiment of camel's hair, and a leathern girdle about his loins; and his meat was locusts and wild honey. Then went out to him Jerusalem, and all Judaea, and all the region round about Jordan, and were baptized of him in Jordan, confessing their sins." Matthew 3:1-6.

Why did Jesus say that it was necessary for Him to be baptized by John?

"Then cometh Jesus from Galilee to Jordan unto John, to be baptized of him. But John forbad him, saying, I have need to be baptized of thee, and comest thou to me? And Jesus answering said unto him, Suffer *it to be so* now: for thus it becometh us to fulfill all righteousness. Then he suffered him." Matthew 3:13-15.

NOTE: *Jesus had not sinned. He did not need to be baptized. In this statement He showed that He wanted to leave us a perfect example of righteous living. He was to do everything* *that was expected of Christians so that they might safely follow in His steps.*

How was Christ baptized by John?

"And it came to pass in those days, that Jesus came from Nazareth of Galilee, and was baptized of John in Jordan. And straightway coming up out of the water, he saw the heavens opened, and the Spirit like a dove descending upon him." Mark 1:9, 10.

NOTE: This text definitely shows that Christ was baptized by immersion in the river for "he came up out of the water."

How did Peter tell the people on the Day of Pentecost that they should demonstrate their repentance?

"Then Peter said unto them, Repent, and be baptized every one of you in the name of Jesus Christ for the remission of sins, and ye shall receive the gift of the Holy Ghost." Acts 2:38.

NOTE: The Greek word used by the New Testament writer in this text is "baptizo," which means to immerse, to dip under, and/or cover with a fluid. It is a transliterated word taken from the Greek language and does not mean sprinkle or pour. When Peter said to those people, "Repent and be baptized," they under-stood him to say. "Repent and be immersed."

In the story of the Ethiopian treasurer, how did Philip baptize him?

"And the angel of the Lord spake unto Philip saying, Arise, and go toward the south unto the way that goeth down from Jerusalem unto Gaza, which is desert. And he arose and went: and, behold, a man of Ethiopia, an eunuch of great authority under Candace queen of the Ethiopians, who had the charge of all her treasure, and had come to Jerusalem for to worship, was returning, and sitting in his chariot read Esaias the prophet. Then the Spirit said unto Philip, Go near, and join thyself to this chariot. And Philip ran thither to *him*, and heard him read the prophet Esaias, and said, Understandest thou what thou readest? And he said, How can I, except some man should guide me? And he desired Philip that he would come up and sit with him. The place of the scripture which he read was this, He was led as a sheep to the slaughter; and like a lamb dumb before his shearer, so opened he not his mouth: In his humiliation his judgment was taken away; and who shall declare his generation? for his life is taken from the earth. And the eunuch answered Philip, and said, I pray thee, of whom speaketh the prophet this? of himself, or of some other man? Then Philip opened his mouth, and began at the same scripture, and preached unto him Jesus. And as they went on *their* way, they came unto a certain water: and the eunuch said, See *here is* water; what doth hinder me to be baptized? And Philip said, if thou believest with all thine heart, thou mayest. And he answered and said, I believe that Jesus Christ is the Son of God. And he commanded the chariot to stand still: and they went down both into the water, both Philip and the eunuch; and he baptized him. And when they were come up out of the water, the Spirit of the Lord caught away Philip, that the eunuch saw him no more: and he went on his way rejoicing." Acts 8:26-39.

NOTE: *Here again the details indicate that the Eunuch was definitely baptized by immersion.*

How essential is it that a person should be baptized by water?

"Jesus answered, Verily, verily, I say unto thee, Except a man be born of water and *of* the Spirit, he cannot enter into the kingdom of God." John 3:5.

Whom did Jesus say would be saved in the kingdom?

"He that believeth and is baptized shall be saved; but he that believeth not shall be damned." Mark 16:16.

What was Paul told to do when he understood the plan of salvation and Christ's work for him?

"And now why tarriest thou? arise, and be baptized, and wash away thy sins, calling on the name of the Lord." Acts 22:16.

By being baptized the individual shows his faith in what three parts of the sacrifice of Christ?

"What shall we say then? Shall we continue in sin, that grace may abound? God forbid. How shall we, that are dead to sin, live any longer therein? Know ye not, that so many of us as were baptized in Jesus Christ were baptized into his death? Therefore we are buried with him by baptism into death: that like as Christ was raised up from the dead by the glory of the Father, even so we also should walk in newness of life. For if we have been planted together in the likeness of his death, we shall be also *in the likeness* of *his* resurrection: Knowing this, that our old man is crucified with *him,* that the body of sin might be destroyed, that henceforth we should not serve sin." Romans 6:1-6.

NOTE: *This is our outward way of showing our faith in our Saviour's death, burial and resurrection and His ability to save us from our sins.*

What does Paul say that we do when we are baptized into Christ?

"For as many of you as have been baptized into Christ have put on Christ." Galatians 3:27.

Our greatest need is to become one with Christ—to accept Him as our Saviour and let Him live out His life in us. God saw that it would be necessary for sinful man to have a day and an event by which he could definitely break with the old life of sin and start a new life with Christ.

The act of baptism is our outward way of showing God and the world that from this day forward we are determined that God will have all that there is of us. We will from this day live for Him. It is the beginning of a new way of life with Christ as our Redeemer. To the newborn Christian this is the day on which he is joined to Christ. Just as with the bride, the wedding day is the day when she is joined to her husband. At that time she takes upon herself the name of her husband and pledges to live for him the rest of her life, likewise, the Christian can no longer live for self, but must henceforth live for Christ.

"Verily, verily I say unto thee, except a man be born of water and of the Spirit, he cannot enter into the Kingdom of God."

John 3:5

Following Jesus All The Way

One of the most pathetic stories recorded in the Bible is that of the rich young ruler who came to Jesus seeking eternal life. Is this story a reflection of our own experience? You will find the story recorded in Matthew 19:16-22.

The story is beautifully presented in the book *The Desire of Ages,* pages 518-520, in these words: "'And when He was gone forth into the way, there came one running,' and kneeled to Him, and asked Him, Good Master, what shall I do that I may inherit eternal life?' . . .

"This ruler had a high estimate of his own righteousness. He did not really suppose that he was defective in anything, yet he was not altogether satisfied. He felt the want of something that he did not possess. Could not Jesus bless him as He blessed the little children, and satisfy his soul want?

"In reply to this question Jesus told him that obedience to the commandments of God was necessary if he would obtain eternal life; and He quoted several of the commandments which show man's duty to his fellowmen. The ruler's answer was positive. 'All these things have I kept from my youth up: what lack I yet?'

"Christ looked into the face of the young man, as if reading his life and searching his character. He loved him, and He hungered to give him that peace and grace and joy which would materially change his character. 'One thing thou lackest,' He said; 'go thy way, sell whatsoever thou hast, and give to the poor, and thou shalt have treasure in heaven: and come, take up the cross, and follow Me.' . . .

"The very holiness of God was offered to the young ruler. He had the privilege of becoming a son of God, and a co-heir with Christ to the heavenly treasure. But he must take up the cross, and follow the Saviour in the path of self denial. . . .

"He wanted the heavenly treasure, but he wanted also the temporal advantages his riches would bring him. He was sorry that such conditions existed; he desired eternal life, but he was not willing to make the sacrifice. The cost of eternal life seemed too great, and he went away sorrowful: 'for he had great possessions.'"

Too many of us are like the rich young ruler. We long for everlasting life, but we are unwilling to go all the way with Jesus.

How far was Jesus willing to go for us?

"Let this mind be in you, which was also in Christ Jesus: Who being in the form of God, thought it not robbery to be equal with God: but made himself of no reputation, and took upon him the form of a servant, and was made in the likeness of men: And being found in fashion as a man, he humbled himself, and became obedient unto death, even the death of the cross." Philippians 2:5-8.

What is the first step we must take to be saved?

"And brought them out, and said, Sirs, what must I do to be saved? And they said, Believe on the Lord Jesus Christ, and thou shalt be saved, and thy house." Acts 16:30, 31.

How earnest must be our desire to become righteous?

"Blessed are they which do hunger and thirst after righteousness: for they shall be filled." Matthew 5:6.

When only will we find God?

"Then shall ye call upon me, and ye shall go and pray unto me, and I will hearken unto you. And ye shall seek me, and find *me,* when ye shall search for me with all your heart." Jeremiah 29:12, 13.

When the man in the parable found a great treasure, how much was he willing to sacrifice to secure it?

"Again the kingdom of heaven is like unto treasure hid in a field; the which when a man hath found, he hideth, and for joy thereof goeth and selleth all that he hath, and buyeth that field. Again, the kingdom of heaven is like unto a merchant man, seeking goodly pearls: who when he had found one pearl of great price, went and sold all that he had, and bought it." Matthew 13:44-46.

When a person finds the wonderful treasure of salvation, how much should he be willing to sacrifice to obtain it?

Your answer:

What does Jesus say of one who lets a loved one keep him from being a Christian?

"And a man's foes *shall be* they of his own household. He that loveth father or mother more than me is not worthy of me: and he that loveth son or daughter more than me is not worthy of me." Matthew 10:36, 37.

What did Jesus say about the individual who is unwilling to leave all for Him?

"And he that taketh not his cross, and followeth after me is not worthy of me." Matthew 10:38.

How far must we be willing to go for Jesus?

"And he said to *them* all, If any *man* will come after me, let him deny himself, and take up his cross daily, and follow me." Luke 9:23.

What kept the rulers of Christ's day from accepting Him?

"Nevertheless among the chief rulers also many believed on him; but because of the Pharisees they did not confess *him*, lest they should be put out of the synagogue: for they loved the praise of men more than the praise of God." John 12:42, 43.

What kept the rich young ruler from following Jesus all the way?

"Jesus said unto him. If thou will be perfect, go *and* sell that thou hast, and give to the poor, and thou shalt have treasure in heaven: and come *and* follow me. But when the young men heard that saying, he went away sorrowful: for he had great possessions." Matthew 19:21, 22.

When we have started on the way with Jesus, what should we purpose to do?

"Ye therefore, beloved, seeing ye know *these things* before, beware lest ye also, being led away with the error of the wicked, fall from your own steadfastness. But grow in grace, and *in* the knowledge of our Lord and Saviour Jesus Christ. To him *be* glory both now and for ever. Amen." 2 Peter 3:17, 18.

What will be our happy experience if we walk in the light which God has caused to shine on our pathway?

"If we say that we have fellowship with him, and walk in darkness, we lie, and do not the truth: but if we walk in the light, as he is in the light, we have fellowship one with another, and the blood of Jesus Christ his Son cleanseth us from all sin." 1 John 1:6, 7.

What wonderful promises are made to us if we follow Jesus all the way?

"Then answered Peter and said unto him, Behold, we have forsaken all, and followed thee; what shall we have therefore? And Jesus said unto them, Verily I say unto you, that ye which have followed me, in the regeneration when the Son of man shall sit in the throne of his glory, ye also shall sit upon twelve thrones, judging the twelve tribes of Israel. And every one that hath forsaken houses, or brethren, or sisters, or father, or mother, or wife, or children, or lands, for my name's sake, shall receive an hundredfold, and shall inherit everlasting life." Matthew 19:27-29.

Are you willing to follow Jesus all the way?

Your answer:

God will not accept a halfhearted surrender. Jesus said that it is impossible to serve two masters. Paul became a great Christian because he followed Jesus all the way. When he was persecuting the Christians, he was the most diligent persecutor the church had; but when he became a Christian, his consecration was just as great. The true Christian will be willing to do anything God indicates.

Abraham of old is called the father of the faithful. He was willing to do everything God commanded him to do. It is said of him in Genesis 26:5, "Abraham obeyed My voice, and kept My charge, My commandments, My statutes, and My laws." When God asked Abraham to take his son and offer him as a sacrifice, he did not hesitate to follow God's command. Taking his son and two servants, Abraham set out for the place appointed for the sacrifice. Arriving at the mountain the third day, Isaac asked, "Behold, the fire and the wood: but where is the lamb for a burnt offering?" Genesis 22:7. Abraham told the lad that God would provide the lamb for the burnt offering. Abraham did not know how he would be able to carry out God's command, but he had faith to believe that God would provide a solution. He would not withhold anything from God, so complete was Abraham's surrender. God honored his dedication and provided a sacrifice so that Abraham could obey God's command and at the same time have his son alive.

Let us trust God. Let us not be afraid to do His will, to keep His commandments—the will of Christ. He makes Himself responsible for our welfare. If, when we have been disobedient, God has cared for us, is He likely to fail us when we step out to obey Him?

In this solemn moment, may we invite you to bow your head and tell the Lord you will follow Jesus all the way. Tell Him, in your own way, that you surrender fully to do His will. Put your hand in the hand of Jesus to go all the way with Him.